EXTINCTION EVENT

THE ALTERED EXPERIENCE BOOK III

EXTINCTION EVENT

MARIA DEVIVO

4 Horsemen
Publications, Inc.

Published By: 4 Horsemen Publications, Inc.

4 Horsemen Publications, Inc.
PO Box 417
Sylva, NC 28779
4horsemenpublications.com
info@4horsemenpublications.com

Cover Illustration by CD Corrigan
Typesetting by Autumn Skye

Library of Congress Control Number: 2024945997

Paperback ISBN-13: 979-8-8232-0641-9
Hardcover ISBN-13: 979-8-8232-0642-6
Audiobook ISBN-13: 979-8-8232-0644-0
Ebook ISBN-13: 979-8-8232-0643-3

DEDICATION

For Joe—Thank you for being my everything. Through any and all pandemics.

For Tina—My sweetest rock of support. You got me through so much, you have no idea.

For Morgan—It's always for you, and always will be for you.

CONTENTS

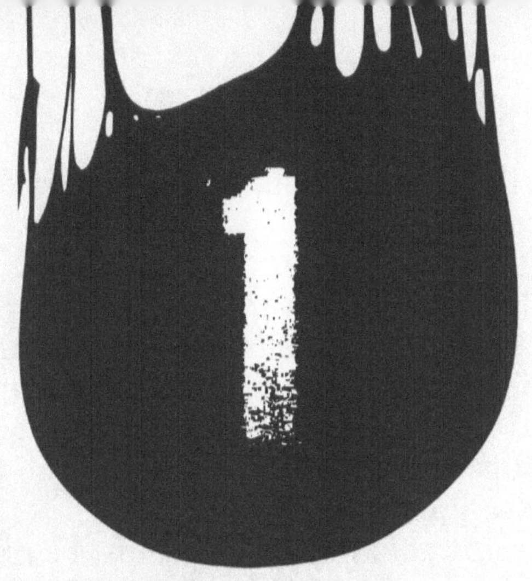

JARROD TWITCHES IN HIS SLEEP. IT'S VIO-lent and jarring, and something I noticed about him right away. I wonder what types of dreams he has when he closes his eyes and travels off to Dreamland. Are they of his past? His present? His future? Any com-bination of the three would be enough to shake his body something awful on a nightly basis, I suppose. I also sup-pose I wouldn't notice it so much if I didn't have to sleep in the same proximity as him. Yeah, right... sleep. Sleep has become something of a memory from long ago. It's been hard for me to find any rest or comfort these last few weeks, and a part of me resents Jarrod for being able to partake in that coveted nighttime ritual—makes me almost glad that his is disturbed by seizure-like body tremors.

Keep on dreaming there, Big J. Keep fighting your demons—the real ones and the make- believe ones. I'll be happy sitting right over here with my back up against the headrest in this abandoned speedboat, suffocating under the black tarp.

A low rumble rises from my stomach, and I freeze, trying to suppress the sound—the feeling. My mouth is dry, and I'm thirsty. Yeah, that's all. Just thirsty. No hunger here.

I could only be so lucky.

Things happened pretty quickly when we arrived on the pier. I guess it didn't take too long for the world to shatter to pieces again. I surmise I was held prisoner on Plum Island for about two months, and the second outbreak and subsequent chaos happened at the same time as my imprisonment.

Second outbreak. Dr. Holston must be rolling over in his grave. I feel like I failed him. "Watch over the Altered," he said. "Don't let Trager get his hands on my research," he said. And look what happened. The world spiraled out of control on my watch. But, I mean, I can't say I didn't try. I did try. Truly and sincerely. I tried to keep Amber safe, Eugene and his band of wretched Ferals safe, and Troy safe.

Troy—the platinum-haired child with the golden sheen skin, the aberration and the anomaly, and quite possibly the answer to this whole mess of a world. He has such a light and a spirit unrivaled by anyone. Being with him was like being with family. It was like being home. Holston had made it a point to tell me to protect him, and in my defense, I tried. Am trying. Because I have to somehow get back to Florida and get to him.

But Florida feels like a universe away. Jarrod and I have roamed and scavenged for a couple of weeks now, and Jarrod says we're in a town called Southold. What do I know? I have to take his word for it. We could be in Timbuktu for all I know. At this pace, it would take me years to get to Tampa on foot. I'm hoping that us "laying low" is going to be a temporary thing, though. Jarrod and I both agreed that we shouldn't get a car until we reach the interstate. Once we get close to I-95, it's a straight shot down to Florida, but for now, we need to "lay low." And it does make sense to lay low because this group of new Infecteds travel in packs—much different from the Infected of the first outbreak.

Almost everything seems to be different from the first outbreak, but then again, I had shelter and security then. I wasn't in the heart of it all; I wasn't in the thick of it like I am now. I had food and water back then. I had the company of my mother, sister, and Toby Youngblood. We were fortified. Protected. And had I just held out a little bit longer, we all would have been okay. But no. Me and my stupid plans had to go and ruin a good thing. Got my sister, my mother, and Toby killed, and me turned. And that's when the real fun started, wasn't it?

Yeah, there's no other way to describe it this time. It's just *different*. The rules have changed. And not just with the Infected. My kind wasn't around back then. There were no Altereds roaming about. And the people? Well, the majority of them had been completely taken off guard, which only added intensity to the chaos. But now? It's as if most had anticipated another outbreak. They were ready. Alert. Prepared. I surmise many people are hiding out in their homes and waiting for the cavalry to come, much like they did last time. But I fear it's not so simple—see, the situation is the same, and yet it's somehow evolved, transformed, taken on a new shape, tone, and identity. Jarrod may be hot-headed and quick-tempered, but he does have his moments of clarity—when the insanity empties out of his brain and the cloud of anger drifts away from his eyes.

"We can't trust the people," he had said the first night we made it ashore and took shelter in some elaborate backyard jungle gym. He pointed to the scar on his cheek. "We can't trust people, because they won't ever trust *us*."

I had nodded in agreement. "Even in an apocalyptic world, we're still public enemy number one."

We hadn't come across any people, though. Heard them, saw them in the distance as we traversed the wooded areas "laying low," but hadn't encountered any, which was probably for the best. Long Island's North Shore has many secluded, little hamlets with expensive homes, lots of land, and beaches on both sides of you. Main Road is literally just that—the main road that cuts straight through the whole island. Jarrod and I stuck to Main Road but always walked parallel to it, never directly on it.

The other day we came upon this old shed behind one of those mom-and-pop breakfast cafés. Jarrod had been mentioning that he wanted to not just "lay low" but to stop and "have peace" for a few days. I, of course, didn't want to stop, but I wasn't going to leave him, and, quite honestly, I didn't want to be alone. So, we made a deal— if I agreed to hang out for a few days, he'd come with me to the interstate and help me get a car.

I don't seem to have much luck with cars, though.

There are tons of Infected everywhere, but we've managed to stay out of their way. It seems as if most of Southold has either left or turned. During the day, we raid the surrounding houses for whatever food and supplies we could get and then came back to the shed at night to sleep. It's a pretty decent plan, considering we're up against two threats—the Infected and the humans. And besides, no human in their right mind would choose to sleep in this dingy shed in this dingy speedboat, propped up on giant cinder blocks under this dingy black tarp.

I would assume they would prefer the soft beds of the mansion homes by the shore, which is exactly why we can't go there. Like I said, Jarrod may be a loose cannon, but he does have his flashes of sanity.

The nights have been getting colder, and while covering ourselves with the tarp makes the air thick and hot, it provides an extra layer of protection from the cold. I'm a pretty light sleeper, so anytime there's a movement from outside, or Jarrod's dreams take him to twitchy places, my head shoots up at attention, and I'm tuned into my surroundings. Having super Altered senses is sometimes a plus.

Jarrod's body eases up on its frenzied spasms, and I let my shoulders sink down a bit. There's howling coming from outside. Whether it's the wind or the Infected doesn't really matter. It sounds soft and comforting. Everything inside the shed is still, and I breathe in deeply. It's nice to just relax for a moment. It's nice to just close my eyes and cock my head back. It's nice to just turn off and tune out. Sleep may very well be in my near future...

Jarrod's body twitches again, and I am roused from my dreamless sleep. I couldn't have been asleep for long because it's still dark out. No light trickles into the shed. No light illuminating the black tarp to a golden gray to signify morning. Jarrod is in the same position as he was before—knees curled to his chest, mouth opened along the ridge of his knee cap. He looks peaceful—too peaceful to have had a quivering moment in a dream. A shuffling noise perks my ears to attention, and another twitch rocks the boat. Only this time, it's an actual rocking and not Jarrod's nocturnal seizure. I freeze under the tarp, not even allowing my eyes to blink, and I listen to the shuffling get louder and closer. I extend my leg and nudge Jarrod's knees. He opens his eyes lazily, and I put my finger to my lips, indicating the urgency to be silent. He nods and twists and turns his body into a sitting position.

He mouths to me, "Infected?"

I shrug my shoulders. I don't think it could be Infected because I distinctly remember locking the shed door before we got under the tarp, at least I think I did. My fear is that it's scavengers like us. People. People looking for supplies or shelter or both.

An arm bobs over the tarp in an unnatural way, and Jarrod's eyes go wide. Bodies crash into the speedboat, jolting us again. Real people don't bumble around like that.

He nods at me and mouths, "Infected."

I nod back, and an eerie sense of calm comes over me. Infected I can handle. Infected don't eat the Altered. Our blood is no good to them; it has too many traces of chemicals and medication—much like feeding processed food to a person who is only accustomed to eating straight from a farm. No, they'll try to come at us, but in the end...

My thoughts stop. *In the end, what?* The rules have changed. The game is different. Can the Infected turn us Altered back? What strand of the Zorna virus runs through *their* veins? Suddenly, I'm not so calm about my chances.

Jarrod mouths, "How many?" and I cock my head to the side, listening, tracking their sounds and movements, trying to get a sense of what we're up against. There's a handful in the shed. I hold up five fingers to answer, but then one of them moans, and that sets them off into a chorus of agony. One by one, they all join the song until the shed and the night air is filled with their dirge. And then I can't tell how many there are because Infected voices surround the structure, surround the speedboat. Jarrod makes a gulping noise in his throat, and I ease back the tarp to peek my eye through the small opening.

They are everywhere.

We're surrounded by a horde.

"We don't know if they can re-infect us," he whispers.

Because we're not like the others. More Altered than Altered.

"We're just gonna have to make a break for it," I say out loud. Who cares who hears us now? There are close to fifty Infected people surrounding us, I think the jig is pretty much up at this point.

"Not without taking some of those bastards out!" Jarrod responds. "There are shovels on the wall. I can position myself on the front of the boat and lean far enough over. You just gotta distract some of them away."

"So what? You're gonna slice heads off with a shovel? This isn't a movie, Jarrod. It doesn't work like that."

He narrows his eyes. "Do you wanna get the hell out of here or not?"

"Are you kidding me?" I say in disbelief.

"Okay then, distract them."

Jarrod pulls the tarp off us, and I help him blanket some of the Infected on the side of the boat. He springs up to the front end of the boat and holds onto the metal railing around the edges. The Infected below go wild at the sight of us and paw at him like revelers at a rock concert. I reach down to grab the tarp and start fanning it up and down, hoping to draw their attention away from him, but as I look up, my heart nearly stops as a parade of Infected steadily files in through the doors. I know the only way out is through them, and I'm not sure if I'll be able to make it through the barrage unscathed.

"We gotta get to the café. Upstairs. Until they wander away," I yell out over the hymn of the damned.

A shovel lands at my feet. "Yep. My thoughts exactly. You ready?"

Jarrod hoists his shovel over his shoulder like a battle sword ready for action. A maniacal grin spreads across his face. I bend down to pick up my weapon and steady it in my hands. The ghost white eyes of the Infected below me burn holes in my memory, and a wave of sickness lurches in my stomach as I realize—*I don't want to kill them*. I was *them* once. I could have easily been killed as well. They didn't ask for this. They didn't want this. And most importantly, they're still in there somewhere—somewhere fighting between the dream and the reality, somewhere fighting between the hunger and the pain, somewhere fighting between the animal urges and the human rationale. They are me, and Jarrod, and Amber, and Eugene, and Crystal, and hundreds of others.

Amber...

An Infected woman with short, curly black hair comes into view, and I immediately think of her. How I left her in that dilapidated house with Eugene and the Ferals. How her hazy, Infected eyes told me that she wanted to be like that—wanted to be in that manic state for the rest of her life. That the world wasn't good enough to have her sane. That it was her destiny to end up that way. That she was going to do as she pleased, no matter what.

Jarrod screams out in pain. An Infected has pulled his leg out and chomped on his ankle. Without hesitation, I swing my shovel against the back of its head, and it crumples to the ground.

Fear paralyzes me. That one bite may have lost me my companion because we're still unsure as to how our bodies will react. "You okay?" I manage to yell.

"Yeah, yeah." He shrugs and curses under his breath. "Griffin, we gotta make our move soon. Kill as many as you can!"

He's right. The line of the damned is getting longer and longer by the second. "I hear ya," I say, as I raise my shovel and bring it down on the neck of an Infected.

We jump down from the boat and slash our way through the pack. Necks snap before me. Hands claw at my sides. Their moans fill the shed and my ears. Their song touches my soul, and a deep part of me is saddened by all this. I wish I could reach out and tell them how very sorry I am for what I have done and what I have to do.

But their movements change when Jarrod passes through the throng. It's as if they don't see him or don't want him. They seem to go the other way.

Before I can tell Jarrod what I notice, one of them tears a chunk of my forearm off with her teeth. She sucks at the open wound as I scream in agony and jerk free from her bite. Blood gushes down my arm like an opened font, and I stumble from the pain. The Infected scrunches her nose as she licks my blood from her lips and turns away from me. *In disgust.*

Jarrod roars with laughter as he kicks another Infected to the ground and plunges his shovel into the base of his skull. He had his back to Jarrod and was walking away, but Jarrod attacked anyway.

"Guess we got our answer!" he screams above their moans.

I drop my shovel and clamp my hand over my wound. "Go! Run!" I yell back.

"Why? What's your rush, man? They don't want us! You see that?" Jarrod swings his shovel at the face of another Infected. It pierces the flesh of the cheek, splitting it wide open, exposing teeth from the side view. It reminds me of Pearl, the Infected woman I watched years ago from the second-story window in my parents' house.

Jarrod catches his breath and smiles at me. "We're more infected than they are, Griffin! That's right!" He screams at the horde. "You got nothing on us, you bastards! We're more infected than you are. You don't want us." He strikes at a different Infected as he chants those words and clears a path from the shed to the café.

When I hold my arm up like a bloody warning sign, the Infected turn the other way. They won't touch me when I'm bleeding like this. They don't even want to look at me. I'm a monster to them. I imagine my infection must smell rancid to their super-heightened senses. The blood continues to pump from my forearm, and I am dizzy, on the verge of passing out, but I manage to stay behind Jarrod as he slashes through a line of Infected like some crazed berserker.

One by one, the bodies of the fallen drop beside me. And one by one, I silently say, "I'm sorry."

W E MAKE OUR WAY INTO THE LITTLE, OLD café. I bust off the lock of the front door with my shovel, and once we're inside, Jarrod drags a chair over to secure it shut.

"Help me with this," he says, and I assist him with piling up the small round tables and other metal chairs from the dining section. Not sure how much help I am because my arm throbs from the bite, and it's hard to move around. The bleeding has eased up some, but the pain is still there. I know I need to get it taken care of soon, or else another type of infection could set in, and I'm not sure if I could bounce back from that. Jarrod hobbles from the bite on his ankle, but overall, he and I are okay. We'll live, if this is what you call living.

I fumble around in the dark, rummaging behind the main counter, looking for something—anything. Gauze, bandages, peroxide. There's nothing here but receipts and some cash. Jarrod barrels through the double doors that lead back to the kitchen. He bumps into something that crashes to the floor, and he curses loudly.

"Shhhh!" I yell, reminding him to be quiet.

He ignores me. "I know this place," he shouts through the opening of the pass-through. "Came here a few times when I was a kid. Good pancakes. The owners transformed their old farmhouse into a restaurant. They lived upstairs or something."

I look up and around. A staircase to the left of me will take us there. "Good to know. Let's go find a bathroom."

By the looks of the upstairs apartment, whoever left this place left in a hurry. A frenzy. Clothes are scattered throughout the rooms, closet doors haphazardly flung open. Whatever happened must have happened quickly and violently.

When I enter the bathroom, a burst of cold air blasts in my face. A broken window lets the wind rush through with a screeching sound.

A faint light flickers behind me in the doorway. "You found the bathroom; I found the flashlight," Jarrod says, as he shines a thin ray under his chin. Shadows dance across his smiling cheeks, giving his face a ghoulish visage.

"Point that thing over here," I plead with him like pleading with a child. He obeys, and I open the vanity under the sink. "Jackpot!" I say, pulling out the precious items I so desperately need. I toss a roll of unwrapped gauze to Jarrod, and he catches it with one hand.

"I guess whoever abandoned this place didn't need first-aid supplies," he mutters.

He flashes the light down the narrow hallway and into one of the bedrooms.

"Guess not." I stand up, corral the items in my arms, and walk by him, following the light from the skinny black flashlight.

He stops me. "Hey, Griffin, you get bit on your ear or something?"

I pause, puzzled. "Not that I know of. Why?"

"Your ear is bleeding."

"It is?"

"Yeah! Running all down your neck and shit. Can't you feel it?"

I tilt my head, rub my right ear against the top of my shoulder, and pull back to get a glimpse. Sure enough, a dark red streak leaves its mark on my shirt, like black ink smeared on a piece of gray paper. "Weird. I hadn't realized," I start to say, but I feel woozy again, and my legs wobble and dip.

Jarrod's smile erases from his face and, with a sense of urgency, he barks out, "C'mon!"

I rest in a rocking chair in the corner of the bedroom, my head propped up with one of the fancy round pillows from the bed. I squeeze the gauze wrap on my arm and watch the little, tiny droplets of blood seep through the white material. *Part-human, part-zombie, and now part-mummy.* I chuckle out loud. I must still be light-headed because there really isn't anything funny about the situation. I hold my arm up and examine the dressing. It reminds me of the experiments on Plum Island, when Jarrod's sister Margo was bitten by their human friend. They threw her back into Jarrod's cell without cleaning up her wounds. I remember how she held up her forearm to show him what was done to her, and he comforted her and held her in his arms to calm her down. Not me, though. Jarrod ignores me. Not that I would want his comfort or hand-holding anyway.

The scent of mothballs—with undernotes of mold— wafts in the room as Jarrod rifles through what's left in the dresser drawers and closet. It's mostly old lady clothing, but there are a few bulky items that I'm sure we could use along the way. He throws heavy sweaters and pullovers onto the queen-sized bed and mumbles something about the cold and the night, protection and batteries. I don't have the head for it all, to be honest. I really need to get some sleep—some real, actual sleep before I can worry about our next move or where we're headed.

Jarrod pulls a sleeping bag from the top shelf of the closet and throws it to the floor with a thud. My eyes had just closed for some rest but were startled wide open.

"This flashlight is gonna die, Griffin."

I sigh. "So let it die."

That's certainly not the only thing that's gonna.

"I found these candles in the old lady's sitting room. I'm gonna light them."

I sigh again and roll my eyes. "I don't think that's such a good idea."

"Why not? We're on the second floor. And the horde wants nothing to do with us. It's fine. I really need to see what I'm getting into over here."

Of course. He slept for a good six hours before we were attacked and after his Infected killing spree, he's got nothing but adrenaline racing through his veins.

"People?" I remind him.

He puckers his lips together and blows out. Saliva droplets spray the air and swirl around in the ray of the Maglite. "Ain't no one around, Griffin. It'll be fine, I swear."

I don't have the energy to debate or argue, so I wave my hand in the air, giving him freedom to do whatever he wants. As if he needed my permission or approval. And so, Jarrod lights three candles in the old lady's bedroom. The light from the tips of the flames dances wildly throughout the room—it mirrors the frantic movements of Jarrod's raid. I close my eyes and prop my chin in the hand of my good arm.

"What do you think we are?" I ask, but the sound of my voice startles me. That was supposed to be an inside thought that escaped while I must have been falling asleep.

Jarrod stops rummaging and looks over at me. "What do you mean?"

"What are we? What did Dr. Rennard and Dr. Trager turn us into?"

His face darkens, and he feverishly rubs his nose. "Killing machines, I guess. I mean, think about it. How long did they have us locked up there? One, two months?"

"About two. Maybe more. Who knows?"

"Maybe more. And every day—every single god-forsaken day—they stuck me with something—probably that Zombaxin, made me look at some whacky pictures, or shoot a gun, or..."

I freeze, and an odd, eerie feeling comes over me. "Shoot a gun? They never made me shoot a gun."

He cocks his head to one side. "No? Hmm." He scratches his head. "Weird. They had me do some crazy target practice a bunch of times."

I remain silent, thinking back to the experiments they put me through.

"The point is—they created us."

"Did they?" I ask, and Jarrod's mouth twists in confusion. A conversation I had with his sister Margo comes back to me, and I remember where he came from, what his mental state was like when he was kidnapped and taken to Plum Island. Margo and Jarrod were Ferals— Altereds who had been left to the streets, the ones who never got therapy at the Re-Assimilation Centers.

He couldn't wait to be infected again. Said he wanted to mess people up real bad and stuff. He said he wanted to OD on Zombaxin so he would be permanently infected again. He said he didn't care if it came down to killing Blake and Kate, cause he was starting to hate them anyway, to be honest. Hated all people. Looked at them as cows. He was filled with so much rage and hate against everyone—humans, Black Bloods...

Amber wanted to be permanently infected again, too. Her eyes had told me that truth. Her crystal blue eyes, washed over with white infection, begged me to leave her be, to let her stay that way, to set her free to wreak havoc on the world she had grown to hate so much. It occurs to me that I could never let Jarrod know that I had been to the Re-Assimilation Center—that I have been his version of "saved," that I was what he called a Black Blood, or what Eugene and his crew called a RAT. There's no telling how his attitude toward me would change, and I'm not willing to find out what it's like on the receiving end of his shovel.

"Those guards..." he continues.

"Good ole Galloway and Davis," I chime with a smile.

He smiles wide again. "We messed them up something awful!"

Actually, you took down Galloway, and Galloway ate her partner after she turned.

"Sure did," I feign agreement. Regardless of who did what, I certainly can't deny the hell that was unleashed on those two humans.

"And it was just the bites. I chewed that one up and spit her out. Altereds can't infect humans, but we did."

"I infected Trager. In all those experiments they did on us, they were giving us the virus, or something along the lines of it," I say, remembering Dr. Rennard's speech to me in the cell on Plum Island. "They were developing it, testing it on us. That doctor said it was a super concentrated form of Zombaxin. *Zombaxin Plus* I believe were her exact words."

"When did that bitch tell you all this? I don't remember her saying that."

"How could you?" I chide. "You were ranting and raving like a lunatic!"

He shrugs his shoulders casually. "Meh, you're probably right."

I shake my head at his dismissive demeanor. "That stuff they sold to people on the black market, that stuff they called Black Death—that was Zombaxin, but it was diluted. It gave Altereds a temporary high, a temporary turn-back, so to speak. And humans who took it got the same rush. It was laced with other drugs, though, to make it addictive. The new Zombaxin, though, that stuff was instant. And whatever it did, it changed the game." I pause and think about my experience with Black Death. It had affected Amber much differently than it had affected me. "Drugs are tricky. There never is a definitive outcome to any drug-induced situation."

"Altereds could now turn humans with the new Zombaxin."

"Pretty much," I agree.

"And this Zombaxin Plus? That's probably what they injected us with every day."

"I'd bet my life on it. That's why we're not crazy Infected like those out there. That's why we're Altered, but can bite and change humans..."

"Think we can change other Altereds?" he whispers in a low voice, as if there's anyone around who can hear.

You'd like that, wouldn't you? I want to say, but don't. I just shrug my shoulders, but I'm guessing he's right. Trager wanted us this way. Lucid, but dangerous. Not like the mindless, instinct-only Infecteds roaming around the city streets. He wanted thinking, feeling, order-taking soldiers who could bring cities to their knees with the slightest bit of saliva.

Jarrod rubs his hands together like a giddy child on Christmas. "Think about it!" he gushes. "We're like the generals in an army of Infecteds. We're the higher breed. The dominant species!"

"And this makes you ... what? Proud? Happy?"

"Justified," he says with finality. "Like, everything I've gone through was for something. Everyone I lost, every person I ate, all the torture on Plum Island was for something. Made me who I am right now."

I raise my eyebrows. "The ultimate killing machine?"

He nods his head. "Ain't that the truth."

Hearing those words solidifies the notion that my time with him will come to an end eventually. Soon. I know it. He and I are just too different to ever see eye to eye for real. Sure, we have a common background, common "ancestry" so to speak, but that's about as far as our friendship goes (if you could even call it a friendship). I'm just a means to his end, and he's a means to my end; the only question mark is whose end will happen first? A part of me rages and screams to myself on the inside to get away from this lunatic—to sneak off in the middle of the night and create as much distance between us as I can. But then, there's another, quieter, gentler voice that whispers, "I'm not done with Jarrod just yet." My stomach growls again.

Jarrod raises his eyebrows. "Whoa! Was that from you?"

"Yeah," I answer sheepishly.

"Hungry much?"

"No!" I snap and swallow hard.

Jarrod plops down onto the bed, covering himself in a sea of women's clothing. He outstretches his arms above his head and yawns loud and deep. I close my eyes and watch the dance of the candlelight flitter shadows across my closed lids.

"You enjoyed killing those people, didn't you?" I say. It was really more of a statement than a question, because I kinda already know the answer.

"They weren't people, Griffin," he defends, but there's a slight uptick in the tone of his voice. Any normal person wouldn't have picked up on the inflection, but my Altered 2.0 senses honed right in on it, so I probe.

"Yes, they were infected, but you were infected once too."

I hear him get up from the bed and blow out the candles. All goes pitch black behind my eyes. "Correction. *Am* infected. I'm more infected than infected. You are, too, and don't you forget it."

"You know what I mean..."

"Look, all I know is this—we are untouchable. We are gods."

There's a calmness in his voice that is haunting. I want to go at him, dispute his godly claims, but the beginnings of a heavy sleep start to work its way up my body. One by one, my body parts go limp, and I start to drift off. "All *I* know is we gotta keep moving. Gotta get out of here. Gotta get back to Florida."

"Soon enough," he says with a yawn. And that's the last thing I hear before I fall asleep.

W E SECURED THE CAFÉ AS BEST WE COULD with whatever materials we could find. The last few days have been uneventful in terms of run-ins with the Infected. Jarrod seems to think that when our blood got in the grass and around the house the other night during the horde attack, it acted as a deterrent to the others. He could be right. When I held out my bloody arm during the attack, the Infecteds practically cleared a path for me. Or was that because of Jarrod's shovel-wielding show? Who knows? Who cares? All I know is that I've had secure peace for at least three days, plenty of food, and a chance to take care of my wound in a sterile environment.

Conversation? Well, that's a whole other issue. Jarrod isn't one for much of it. We talk about surface things like, "Do you want to eat the can of cherry pie filling or blueberry pie filling today?" or, "Which parka do you think goes with these jeans?" or, "Do you think we'll need to pack this spool of rope for the road?' Stupid stuff. Trivial stuff. Not a lot of substance stuff, if that makes sense. I'm not sure if he's capable of having a deep conversation or if he just doesn't want to open up. That's weird to me—you live on the road with someone, have the same historical experiences with someone, kill people with that person, and the farthest you get in your intimate dialog is whether or not you want to light candles in the dark? I don't know. I don't get it. Maybe it's just me, though. Maybe I expect more from humanity. Maybe I've expected more since I lost mine. But look who I'm dealing with—Jarrod, an angry Altered, an angry Feral devoid of humanity. Maybe I need to start lowering my expectations.

The broken mirror in the bathroom tells me another story. I've definitely seen better days, that's for sure. I look like I've aged a good ten years. My skin looks like there's a gray filter washing over it, and my eyes look like they're a lighter shade of brown. I guess all the changes my body has gone through are starting to present themselves in a physical aspect. I'm still lean, but I've been that way since the beginning of this mess. I haven't had much of an appetite since I kicked the "eating people" habit a few years back. There was a time, not so long ago, when this reflection would have embarrassed me. Like a spoiled child, I would have locked myself in my room, vowing to never show my face to the world again, fearful that Lana Anderson from my fifth period What-the-Hell class would have laughed at the way I looked. Now, to think back on all that, what's embarrassing to me is the stupid priorities I put so much emphasis on. Lana Anderson is long dead, right along with my buddy Josh, and hundreds of thousands of others.

And the crazy thing about it is—I'm still here. I guess that counts for something.

I could only be so lucky.

In Jarrod's defense, he has helped out a lot with the plan and seems to be sticking to it. He was the one who wanted to stay at the café for a little bit, and I obliged him, but for most of the time, he's been sorting through supplies, making escape packs with provisions from the pantry, small tools, clothes. I hate to say it, but he thinks of more necessary items than I ever could. Kinda like he's done this before. But he has done this before—a version of this, at least. When he and his sister Margo were injected with the serum and Altered, they were left to the streets, left to fend for themselves. Scavenging and surviving were all they knew. I don't think I can blame him for hating my brand of Altered—the brand that got a first-class ticket to shelter, food, medicine, and therapy. Even if the Re-Assimilation Center was a mill in itself and probably not the most ideal situation, it still was safety. And that was something Jarrod and Margo never had.

I often find myself wondering about the people who lived in this apartment before the outbreak. From the décor and the clothing, I can surmise that an older woman resided here, but was she alone? Did she have family? A husband? Children? What kind of person was she? Was she a hardened pessimist or a happy-go-lucky grandma? How did she survive the first outbreak? Jarrod and I had gone through most of the personal items left behind—clothes, bills, paperwork from the café, some jewelry—and he swears the old lady now roams outside on the beaches, singing the song of the Infected. But I say otherwise. She's safe somewhere, I just know it. She left—quickly, but willingly. I can tell. All the picture frames are empty.

Jarrod likes to leave the window open at night and hunker down under a swamp of blankets and clothes, but the last two nights were so brutally cold that I'm going to insist he keep it closed tonight. He's been sleeping in the bed, and I stick with the rocking chair. It's uncomfortable, but at least I'm not woken up by his constant jolting.

"So, we should think about heading out in a couple of days," Jarrod says when he comes into the room.

I nod. "Agreed."

He throws a red sleeping bag into my lap and lights the candles around the room. "That's the last of 'em."

I pick it up, balancing the weight in my hands. "This is a good one."

"That makes six," he says as he opens the window, and a blast of night air surges into the room.

I roll my eyes. I really want to say something about keeping it closed, but hearing how many packs he made distracts me. I shake my head. "Wait. Six? In addition to my two, or total? How are we gonna...?"

"Total. I hooked some rope to the back of two of them. We can fling those on our backs and carry the others under each arm. Until we find a car to use."

"Yeah, and I'm sure owners just leave spare keys behind the passenger seat visors, ya know, just in case of an apocalypse or something. Are we gonna go raid every house and go through every rich lady's pocketbook, looking for the keys to her Lexus? Unless you know how to hotwire..."

Jarrod tilts his head forward and raises his eyebrows. My ears go red, and I shut up. Of course, he knows how to hotwire a car. Jarrod. Margo. Ferals. Survival. I wouldn't know a thing about survival if it bit me on the ass. Hell, I got my family killed and myself infected when I tried to be all hero-like and get my stupid car. I turn my face toward the window and stare out into the dark wilderness.

"I organized everything by days. We barely ate, so I didn't think we needed much food. I got that Maglite, and those batteries we found in the drawer downstairs. I took money out of the register just in case, ya know, if people still care about money and all."

"Medicine," I say. "It'll be all about the medicine. I got all of it in the green pack over there." And I point to the pile in the corner of the room.

"Oh," his voice sounds genuinely surprised. "You mean there was more than just the Tylenol?"

All of a sudden, I see a flicker of light in the distance. A faint flash of light coming from the brush. I pull my body closer to the window sill, ears at attention like a guard dog.

"Griffin, what other medicine was there?" Jarrod repeats.

"Shhhhh," I say, shutting him up. I stare more intently out the window, trying to make sense of the images and shadows lurking in the dark.

Jarrod crouches down low beside me. "What's out there?" he whispers.

A rustling noise twitters close by, and there's movement in the trees of the forest.

"Oh, just the wind," Jarrod says with a dismissive wave of his hand.

But the light glints off the trees again. "No! Look!" I say, and my ears pick up the traces of voices.

"Please. Stop. Don't," a weak voice seems to say as the movements get closer and louder. And then another sound follows it. A familiar sound. A gurgling, bumbling sound. I know Jarrod hears it, too, because we lock eyes with a sense of understanding. We know those sounds too well—the stock plea of a human followed by the merciless retort of the hunter. He clutches the arm of the rocking chair, and his knuckles briefly go white before he hoists himself back up and blows out all the candles in the room.

Two figures soon manifest in the moonlight. Two people running toward the café. Two people with a cluster of Infected right on their heels. I squint my eyes to try to see them better. Blonde hair tangles in the wind. A young boy points and winks at me. Toby and Josh returning from the grave to haunt me. Illusions. Deceptions.

"Shut that window and get low!" Jarrod orders, pulling me out of my trance.

"Toby" stumbles over some bramble, and "Josh" comes to a skidding halt. He pivots his body and extends his hand to help her up. *I guess there's something going on with the two of them. Maybe they met up in the afterlife and talked to each other about how I killed them both.* The Infected get closer to them.

"Wait!" I say. "We gotta help them."

"What?" Jarrod responds in disbelief.

"Help!" the man screams from outside. "I know someone's up there. Please! Help us!"

"They'll die, ya know," I say nonchalantly.

"And?"

The woman screams. The Infected voices get closer, louder.

"And they need our help. What if that was you out there? And Margo?"

Jarrod's face darkens. "It was," he growls.

I don't care what he says. He left the window open too many nights and lit those candles when I told him not to. If Toby and Josh need my help, I have to try to help them. Josh died because of me. Toby died because of me. A lot of people died because of me, and I'm still here. If I can do this one thing...

"They're people. They won't understand..." he calls to my back as I race down the stairs and toward the front door.

God, I have no idea why I stay with him! Understand what? What's there to understand? These people need help. Like, legit help. We're planning on leaving soon, anyway. If Josh and Toby need to stay here for shelter after we're gone, then why not?

I remove the barricades and poke my head into the frigid air. "Here," I whisper, and within seconds, the two of them appear from behind the overgrown floral arch in the front patio. "Quick," I command as I usher them in the front door. The man helps me stack up the blockade again, and the woman stands hunched over, hands on knees, breathing heavily.

"Thank you! Thank you so much," she repeats over and over.

When we're done, the man extends his hand to me. It's cold and caked with dirt and grime, but I clasp it with a friendly shake anyway. Immediately, I'm overcome with a feeling of cold dread. There's something in his eyes, something in his grip that sends a shiver throughout my body when he moves his arm up and down with mine. In the darkness, I see shadows dancing around him, like demons poking out of Pandora's Box. It's been a while since I've been around humans. My memories of them are a bit jaded. I'd forgotten how they all reacted to us

Altered, how they refused to serve Amber Chinese food, how they brutalized us on Plum Island. I swallow hard. The ice chill up my arms confirms to me that Jarrod was right. I think I just let death in through our front door. "Griffin," I say with a croak in my throat.

Josh, I fully expect him to reply. "Matt," he says.

"Charlie," the woman blurts out breathlessly.

Matt jerks his hand away quickly. "You alone?" he asks, shining his flashlight in my face. There's a darkness in his voice that makes the hair on my arm stand at attention, and a prickling in the back of my neck sends an inner "Uh-oh" to my brain.

"No, no," I say quickly, trying to mask my suspicions. "My friend Jarrod is upstairs." *If I could call him that.* "You're not bitten or anything, are you?"

They both shake their heads. "Scraped up my leg when I fell, but I'm okay. That's about it," Charlie says.

I extend my arm out in the direction of the staircase, motioning for them to walk in front of me. "I have some supplies upstairs to clean that up for you if you like."

Charlie smiles and walks past me, but Matt notices my bandaged forearm and puts his arm out to stop her. He raises his eyebrows and nods his long chin at it.

I hold up my arm. "Glass," I say. "Cut it trying to break into this fortress." I chuckle at my lie, and Charlie gives a soft smile and continues up the narrow stairs.

Jarrod stands in the hallway with his arms crossed like a sentry on duty. "Everybody check out okay?" he asks.

"Yeah, all good," I say from behind, and Jarrod leads them into the bedroom. Matt sits on the floor against the dresser, and Charlie positions herself between his legs. Jarrod and I follow in. He takes his normal spot on the edge of the bed, among the stacks of clothes and blankets, and I decide to stay in the doorway.

Jarrod eyeballs me with disdain. It's the same look my mother gave me when I let Toby Youngblood into our home that night during the first outbreak. I know he's angry with me for letting them in, but I felt like I didn't have a choice. I had to do something to help. Josh would have wanted it. Lana and Toby would have wanted it. My mom would have wanted it.

"Thanks for letting us in. We really appreciate it," Matt says, but his voice is coarse and hollow.

Jarrod nods in recognition, and Charlie nuzzles her face in the crook of Matt's neck. "What happened out there?" he asks them.

Matt breathes in, and his body tenses up defensively. "What do you mean? Don't you know? Where have you guys been this whole time? Isn't this your place?"

Jarrod shakes his head. "No, I mean, what happened to *you two* out there."

Matt relaxes a little, pulls the hair away from Charlie's face, and kisses her on top of her head. "It was fast," she mumbles in a faraway voice, as if in deep memory. "Reports. Sightings. Incidents. Our wedding..." She gasps a little in her throat and snuggles so close up against Matt that it looks as if she's actually trying to enter his body.

"You know," he says matter-of-factly.

"No. We actually don't," I blurt out.

Matt looks up at me and raises a suspicious eyebrow. I glance nervously over at Jarrod, and I can tell the wheels in his head are turning something fierce. "Me and Griffin were on Plum Island for a few months. We went off the grid for a little bit, just to get away, ya know?"

"When we got back, everything had gone to hell again," I chime in. Which isn't really a lie.

Matt bites his lower lip and nods his head. "That Black Death," he begins, "and all those conflicting reports. You'd turn on the TV one day, and they said everything was fine and all, and the next it was all doom and gloom. Some reports said there were instances of infection that couldn't be treated with the original Altered serum. They had to put those people down."

"Drugs sure are a tricky thing," Jarrod interrupts and looks to me sharply.

Matt gives him a confused look, but my Altered senses are in overdrive. Matt gave me the creeps from our first handshake, and I know Jarrod is picking up on the same vibe. I nonchalantly walk into the room, reach for the green medicine pack on the clothes pile, and take a seat on my rocking chair. Just in case. Just in case he tries anything funny and tries to rob us blind in the middle of the night. I'm so smooth as I prop my head under the rolled-up sleeping bag that I kind of want to pat myself on the back for being so stealthy.

"Living out here, on east Long Island, sometimes separates you from everything going on," Matt continues. "Shit doesn't seem real sometimes. We were so sure it wasn't gonna happen again. And we were planning our wedding and well, before we knew it, the government was calling for voluntary evacuations."

Evacuations? As in, they had a plan for this? As in, they had anticipated something happening again? "Evacuations? To where?" I ask.

Matt turns his head toward me. "I ... I'm not really sure," he stammers a little. "The high schools, I think. Anyone who wanted shelter had forty-eight hours to get to a Safe Zone. We obviously didn't go. Our whole neighborhood decided to stay back. We thought the coast would be protection enough. Backs against the sea."

"Safe Zone?" I question. "Why not Re-Assimilation Centers?"

Matt blinks his eyes quickly and gives me a suspicious look. "Why would they set up those? There isn't anyone *to* re-assimilate. Like they said, the drugs don't work on these newly infected people."

"Tell me about this Safe Zone," Jarrod interjects, and we glance at each other. Even in the darkness, I can see the worried expression on his face. "What happened after forty-eight hours? If you didn't get there?"

"The phones stopped working first. Then the electricity. The systematic shutdown, one by one, just like the last time. But I was able to ride it out back then, so I wasn't too concerned about this time around, ya know? Then some of the men on the block formed a search-party group to go out into the town and get supplies. Only they didn't come back. Another group organized to go look for the first group, but they didn't come back either." Matt clenches one of his fists, and I sense a dangerous anger rising up inside him.

"Listen," I say, "there's enough supplies here that will last for a little while. Jarrod and I haven't been here long, and we're leaving in a few days. You and Charlie will have this place to yourselves."

"Leaving?" Charlie squeaks into Matt's chest.

"Where are you going?" Matt asks.

"We're getting the hell outta Dodge," Jarrod says. "We're going to Florida. Griffin knows a doctor there."

Matt's spine stiffens, and he plants both hands firmly on the floor, ready to spring up at a moment's notice.

"Doctor? What kind of doctor? What are you talking about? Florida is a long way from New York, man."

I muster the most soothing voice I possibly can use. "Just my cousin." *Lie.* "She's a pediatrician," *not a lie*, "and she helped my family during the first outbreak." *Lie.* "I just think it would be best to be around family during a crisis, and well, having medical expertise is also a plus!" *Sorta a lie, and not a lie.*

"Besides," Jarrod says, forcing a laugh, "it's gonna get real cold real soon up in these northern states. Florida is always warm, even when it's cold."

Matt's body eases up, and he wraps his arms around Charlie's shoulders. He rests his head against the wooden dresser and closes his eyes. "Maybe Florida wouldn't be so bad. Maybe we'll ride with you," he says.

Jarrod's head snaps to my direction. He shakes his head slowly back and forth in an ominous way. He's right. There's no way we can let these two come with us. I'm sorry I even let them in.

D AYLIGHT BARELY MAKES ITS WAY OVER the horizon, and I feel the first budding rays of the sun tingle with warmth on my face through the open window. I was dreaming about something—something good and comforting, something that made me feel happy and good, but the memory of it faded when I was dragged back up into consciousness. I'll just stay here for a few more minutes until the morning is complete. Leaves rustle outside. Birds begin to flitter about. Infected moan in the distance, probably aggravated that they lost their "Matt and Charlie" special. I sense Jarrod's absence in the room and hear rumblings from the pantry beneath us. A cold, metallic object jabs on the side of my face, and a gun hammer clicks loudly near my ear.

I instantly and cautiously open one eye. Matt stands over me with a handgun barrel pressed against my face— under my eye by my Altered scar. My body tenses as I slowly open my other one. "What are you doing?" I manage to mumble, but my voice is so shaky I can barely get the words out.

"Plum Island? Off the grid? I knew your stupid story didn't make sense," he growls at me and digs the gun harder against my cheek. "I thought I recognized your scar last night, but now, in the light…" He spits on the floor. "I bet this all was your fault. You and your friend. I bet you had something to do with all this turning to hell again."

I say nothing. It's better to say nothing when lunatics ramble. It's better to let them get out all of their brain vomit while I formulate the perfect comeback and talk my way out of certain death. But, I'm finding it quite difficult to do with a gun to my face. I look over Matt's shoulder, and Charlie is standing in the bedroom doorway, clutching a large kitchen knife. Suddenly, I think Jarrod is dead—she must have killed him! But then my senses pick up on more movement from downstairs. He has no idea any of this is happening.

"I promise you, Matt," I begin to say calmly, "Jarrod and I had nothing to do with any of this. We really were on Plum Island, I swear." Cause we don't. And we were.

He shoves the barrel into my scar and laughs. "Plum Island? Come on! Everyone who lives out here knows that's an animal sanctuary. No one ever goes out to Plum Island. Especially not to vacation!"

Animal sanctuary? Is that what they tell the locals? I'd like to tell Matt what really happens on Plum Island. As a matter of fact, I'd love to show him even more. "Vacation wasn't a good word. It was more like an adventure. We heard stories, ya know? Jarrod heard rumors. We wanted to see."

Charlie fidgets with the kitchen knife. Her hand rattles back and forth with fear. It's obvious she's uncomfortable holding it, which is unfortunate because she won't last too much longer in this world if she has a problem with defense weapons. Toby would have held that knife properly at least. She might have been a little shaky at first, but she would have known what to do with it. Now Amber ... oh man, Amber wouldn't have even needed that knife. Nope. Amber was a stone-cold killer at heart, even before she was infected and Altered. She had a killer's instinct before, during and after, and she was able to hide it for a decent amount of time—until she got sick of hiding it. Until she was introduced to the Black Death. Until she found a way to go home...

Matt takes a step back and creates a little distance between my cheek and the gun. "Listen, we're taking this place now. Get your friend. Get your stuff. Go where you're planning on going, and start going there *today*..."

He's too involved in the sound of his own commanding voice to hear Charlie's squeals of pain coming from the doorway. But I do. I look over, and Jarrod is behind her with his hand clamped over her mouth. The knife falls to the carpet with a thud, and still Matt is oblivious.

"Put your gun down, or I'll kill your wife," Jarrod says slowly.

Matt stops his tirade and looks over at them. A look of panic spreads across his face.

"Put the gun down," Jarrod repeats. "Let Griffin pass. I'll send her over to you. No one has to get hurt."

Charlie struggles to break free of Jarrod's hold, but it's no use. Matt looks at her worriedly, looks at me, looks at the gun, and hesitantly places it on the floor. I stand up, grab my green medicine pack, and swoop up the gun before Matt changes his mind. Jarrod shoves Charlie into the room and reaches down for the knife. As she passes by me, I inhale her scent. She smells like iron. Like metal. Her smell fills my nostrils and for a second, I breathe the familiar smell in. It's heavenly. Delightful. Makes me sweat a little with excitement. Makes my stomach growl furiously.

Charlie hobbles over to Matt, holding the side of her neck. She throws her body into his arms. "Don't let them take our gun, Matt," she whispers to him.

"You can have this place," Jarrod says to them. "We're leaving."

"Don't take our gun, man," Matt pleads.

"You don't need it," Jarrod says dryly.

"We'll die if we don't have it!" Matt screams.

I walk down the stairs, Jarrod behind me.

"You're already dead," Jarrod says, and then it dawns on me—the metallic smell from Charlie was coming from an open wound. But not any open wound. She was bitten. Jarrod bit her, and the thought of her iron-tasting wound makes my mouth salivate. *What did she taste like? How did she taste? How did it feel to have her warm blood fill his mouth and run down his throat?*

One thing was for sure—she would turn and bite Matt, and Matt would turn, and they would live out the rest of their infected days bumbling about the old café. The cycle would continue.

Now I think I'm starting to understand why I stay with Jarrod—he's able to do the things that I'm not ready, or willing, to do ... *yet.*

He throws three packs at me, and I put one over my shoulder and tuck the other two under my arms.

"And that, my friend, is why we will inherit the Earth," he says, and we both kick the barricade to the front door away and walk out.

"What's the obsession with you and Florida, anyway?" Jarrod asks as we continue to walk down Main Road.

My guard immediately goes up, and I know I have to choose my words carefully when I respond to him. I've told him bits and pieces of the story, altered some facts here and there, but never full disclosure.

"Seriously. You keep mentioning that doctor. How do you know her? How do you know she's even going to help you? What makes you think that there's even help out there?"

"Remember I told you about those guys I hooked up with?"

"The ones who turned you and your girl on to Black Death?"

I nod my head. "Yep."

"And the girl and her weird baby," he continues.

"Well, the weird baby was under Dr. Holston's care, and from time to time, we all took Crystal and Troy to their weird appointments."

"Why, though? And I thought you said Holston died."

"Holston seemed to think that Troy was special. He had been infected when he was in utero and Altered in utero. He wasn't like the rest of us, either. Had a different blood type."

Jarrod's face screws up to one side. "Different blood type? How is that possible?"

I shrug my shoulders. "I don't know. That's just what Holston said. But then, yeah, Holston died. I went to his funeral, ya know, to pay my respects and shit for him taking such good care of Troy. And that's when I met his niece, Dr. Oswald."

Jarrod violently shakes his head. "Nah, man. I wouldn't have paid respects to no one! Especially that old man!" He balls up a fist and is visibly upset. "After what they did to me. To you. We should have killed them all. They treated us like animals; no wonder we got that stupid nickname. *Ferals.* But it's true. They left us out there to die. And why? Cause it took us longer to 'wake up' from that serum?" He punches his fist into his open hand with a loud *cracking* sound. "You're kinda hanging on to some pipe dream, aren't you, Griffin? The great and powerful Dr. Oswald's going to save us all from the apocalypse," he sings in a sarcastic tone. "You're just kidding yourself. What the hell is she gonna do for you? Why should she even care?"

I keep my head focused on the ground and kick away the rocks on the side of the road. I don't know whether or not I want to punch him out for being a non-believer, or high-five him for his realistic perspective. All I can think about is getting to Troy, keeping him safe, and getting someone—anyone—to figure out this mess. But along with Troy comes Crystal and Oswald and Eugene and, dare I say, Dr. Graves? The whole lot of them pulling and tugging at that special child for their own personal gain. What's my motivation? To uphold some promise I made to a dying man?

No. There's more to it.

"I gotta believe that there's help somewhere out there," I say. "Besides, I don't see you with any bright ideas. Look, if you don't want to come with me, I'll be totally okay if you want to bail..."

"No, no, no!" he defensively interrupts. "I'll go with ya. I'm kinda curious to see how this all plays out. And you're right, I don't have a plan. We've made it this far together, why not go the whole nine yards, right?" He forces a smile. "Florida sounds solid. Winters in New

York can be brutal, and I'd rather not be around when it comes."

"Okay," I say and keep walking.

Wanting to reunite with Troy wouldn't be for my own personal gain, per se, but there are some selfish reasons behind why I want to get back to him. When he and Crystal stayed with me for those few days some months ago, I felt whole. And real. Like there was a true purpose in my life. Troy is this amazing beacon of light and life and innocence. Being in his very presence was a magical experience. I didn't feel alone, scared, or unsafe for the first time in a long while. Did Eugene feel the same way about Troy? Did Eugene turn me in to Trager so that he could get Troy and Crystal back? Did Oswald get the same feeling when she met Troy? I remember she was enthralled by his appearance and was eager to run many tests on his blood and hair samples. Did she want to study him and learn from him and keep him for herself, too? She was a pediatric surgeon. I mean, I'm sure there were a ton of things she could do with him. Anger rises up in me when I think of someone betraying me because, ultimately, someone did. Someone knew where I was, when I was, and tipped off Rennard and Trager to come and whisk me away as one of their playthings. My head starts to spin, and my ears get hot. I have to stop thinking about it. I have to change the subject of my internal dialog, or I'll explode.

I start to replay our scenario with Matt and Charlie—what I did wrong, how I didn't trust my instincts. I have to constantly remind myself that the game has changed, but I have, too. There's something inside me that separates me from the others. Not human, not Altered, not Infected. I know that knowledge is power, and, in this world, supplies are power too. I am power, but that's a whole other issue. That's something I'm going to have to come to terms with soon, but right now I need to keep my focus. Keep my eye on the prize and trust my gut. My gut just told me I need more information. I need to know more about what's going on in the world around me. I need to assess the game, so I'm better equipped to play.

"That guy talked about a Safe Zone," I say.

Jarrod narrows his eyes. "A Safe Zone isn't gonna get us to Florida any faster..."

"I know that. But if we found one, hung around for a few days, maybe we could get some info. Who knows? Maybe we could get someone to help us, like the military or something."

Jarrod stops and stares hard at me before bursting out into laughter. "Now I know you're just messing with me! The military! You're a funny guy, Griffin. A real funny guy!"

I shake my head. "I'm not joking, Jarrod."

He pauses and points to the scar under his eye. "You know what this means? It means 'No Altereds Welcome.' If a Safe Zone actually exists, what makes you think they'll even consider letting us in? Over the humans? You heard what Matt said; he thought me and you started this whole thing up again."

"Did we?" I say under my breath.

Jarrod throws his hands in the air in disbelief. "What's wrong with you, man? Why do you always have these crazy ideas?"

"You wanna walk to Florida?" I say sarcastically.

"I told you we would get a car! I can hotwire them!"

"And if there are people and military and a town center or something, maybe that's our chance for getting one! And if anyone knows anything…"

"No one knows anything!" he screams. "Everyone knows what we know. Zombies walked the Earth and wreaked havoc; they were suppressed and changed for a few years; they came back. Period. The end."

Zombies. That's the first time I ever heard him call the Infected that. I hate that word. It sounds so stupid and unreal.

"And besides," Jarrod continues, "didn't Matt say the mandate was forty-eight hours or something? I think we missed the deadline a long time ago."

I can tell I'm not getting anywhere with Jarrod. He needs a little more convincing, and during my time with him, I've pretty much figured where to hit him hardest. "I think it's still worth a shot," I say with conviction. "Any advantage that we could pick up will only help us, not hurt us. We have enough supplies. We have a gun. We have knives." I pause. "And we have these." I point to my teeth. "You said it yourself. We're like gods or something."

His eyes light up.

I'm definitely speaking his language now. Without hesitation, I flip my backpack over my shoulder and quickly find the tourist map of Long Island I took from the café's gift shop. "You know this place better than I do," I say, keeping up my momentum. "Where are we now? Are we still in Southold?"

He nods his head. The glimmer in his eye doesn't fade.

"Oaklawn Avenue," I say. "There's a high school on that road. And an elementary school. And a church."

He nods his head and continues walking.

I follow behind him, and as soon as I do, a long roll of thunder rumbles off in the distance. As if on cue, the sky opens up, and heavy drops of cold rain fall down on us.

Jarrod points to a long row of abandoned cars lined up along the side of the street. "C'mon," he says over a gust of wind.

The two of us scramble to find an unlocked door, and when I do, we both climb into the front seats. We'll have to wait out the rain here. Being wet and cold might put us at a disadvantage, and to be honest, I'm not in the mood to be cold and wet any time soon.

"Let's go right now," Jarrod says.

The rain pounds heavily on the roof of the Toyota like a steel drum echoing in my head. "What are you talking about?"

"I can get this car started, ya know. Why would we even bother going to that Safe Zone? Who's to say it's even safe? Or if it's ever been safe for that matter? I can get this baby fired up right now, and we can cruise on down I-95 like it's nobody's business!"

I shake my head. "No way. I need answers. Confirmation, of sorts. We can get info there, especially if they're government-led."

"Oh yeah? And who the fuck are we? What makes you think anyone is gonna tell us anything? No one owes us! No one gives a shit about us, remember?" He points at his face. To his scar, but he doesn't need to remind me. He doesn't need to call to attention what I know. What kind of asshole does he take me for?

"I don't know! Human nature? Preservation of the species? Simple friggin' compassion, maybe? There are people out there who aren't completely against us, ya know."

He sighs. "Yeah, yeah. Like that doctor friend you're always going on about. Doctor What's-Her-Face."

"Oswald."

"Alright, so refresh my memory. What is so important about that weird kid anyway?"

I pull the sleeves of my shirt over the tops of my hands. "Troy. His name is Troy. I dreamt about him last night, which is weird because I haven't had very many dreams since I was Altered, much less remember them as vividly as this one. The dream wasn't so much *about* him as I *was* him, if that makes any sense. Like I was seeing the dream through his eyes. But he wasn't a little kid. He was all grown up, like my age or something. And he was at a funeral. There were so many people there, and I knew whoever died must have been really important. Troy's mother was there, Dr. Oswald, and so many others. Yet, *I* wasn't there, so I thought that maybe it was *my* funeral. But when I looked down through Troy's eyes and saw the headstone, it was engraved with *Dr. Warren J. Graves*. I guess that's why I wasn't there, because I always hated that fucker."

Jarrod chuckles. "You're one strange dude, Griffin."

"But then me, as Troy, looked beyond the headstone and through this enormous cemetery, all the way to the Brandon Regional Hospital in Florida…"

"The Re-Assimilation Center?"

"Yep. And in front of the hospital is this giant golden statue. Of me. Griffin."

Jarrod lets out a boisterous laugh and nearly chokes on it. "You? A statue of you? What the hell for?"

I shrug my shoulders. "I have no idea."

"Well, what happened next?"

"I woke up."

He huffs. "Ya know, Griffin, I—"

"Just humor me, alright? Come with me to the Safe Zone. Help me find out if there's any merit to getting to Florida. Seriously. If there's nothing to go to, then I guess we could ... I don't know. I just need to know. Something. Anything."

He closes his eyes and cocks his head back on the seat. "Okay, Griffin. We'll stick to your plan. Might as well. I ain't got a better one."

"SEE THAT GUY UP THERE? HE'S GOT A hunting rifle. I know that gun. I think it's a Browning, but I could be wrong. But that other guy, the black dude over on the left, he's got a Henry Big Boy. My dad always wanted me to get a Henry Big Boy." Jarrod nods his head and licks his lips.

I roll my eyes. "I never took you for a hunter."

"Yeah, well, it was more my dad's thing and—"

There's movement on the rooftop of Southold High.

"Shhh," I caution in a hushed tone.

So far we've spotted two armed guards patrolling the rooftop, but soon, a third appears on the far right corner side of the roof. We had cut through the back streets and wandered through the historic Southold Cemetery until we were directly across the street from the high school. It's kinda odd and creepy that they built a high school across the street from the cemetery. I bet it made for interesting field trips! Luckily for us, we're hiding out behind a tree line just outside the fence of the graveyard. Everything is overgrown, and we have a decent amount of coverage.

The school is a red brick building with white columns decorating the main entrance way. It has a colonial, old-school look to it—like something out of the 1940s. My high school in Florida was much more modern-looking with a stark white façade that almost looked like a hospital. The word "Southold" is written in big blocky letters on the front archway of the school, and I smirk to myself. *Old South. South Old. South Hold.* When I think of the Old South, I think of *Gone with the Wind*, or Alabama, or the Louisiana Bayou, not some uppity New York beach town.

"The school seems small for a high school," I whisper.

"There were only like five hundred kids that went here. It was junior and senior high combined."

"Yikes. My high school in Florida had nearly three thousand students!"

"Back in the day, I used to hang out with a chick who went here. Southold's not a big town. The whole north side of the Island is pretty sparse and—"

"Shhh..." I whisper again when I see a fourth guard come into view.

Jarrod inches his body closer against the tree and rests his head on the trunk. He's breathing a little heavier. "Do you think they saw us?"

"No. If they saw us, I think they would have shot at us."

"Yeah. You're right." He relaxes a little. "You get a weird feeling from all this?"

I nod my head. "They don't look military."

"That was the first thing I noticed. Wouldn't they be in uniform or something if this was an official Safe Zone?"

I nod again. "Makes you wonder what happened here."

And I do wonder what happened. Matt said the military called for voluntary evacuations to the Safe Zones.

A military operation like that would have been calculated and organized, armed with trained men. From the looks of it, four guys patrolling the roof of a high school with hunting rifles seems a far cry from a structured setup. I get the feeling that something bad must have gone down here at Southold HS.

"There's only one way to find out," Jarrod says.

We wait until the men on the roof have their backs turned in other directions, and on the count of three, we sprint across the front lawn and up the concrete steps. I never get a chance to pound on the front door because the moment we make it to the top of the staircase, the white door opens, and a rifle pokes its deadly head at us. Instinctively, Jarrod and I drop the packs we're carrying and put our hands up in a "don't-shoot" stance.

"You're on government property, gentlemen," a deep voice booms from within the corridor. "You need to keep on moving. This Safe Zone is filled."

"We just need a place to stay for a few nights. It's just the two of us," I plead.

The figure steps out from behind the door with his rifle still trained on us. His dark hair is shaggy around his face, and his beard is full and scruffy. He's also dressed in full military gear—camo and boots, the whole enchilada. Jarrod and I glance at each other from the sides of our eyes, and while I can't quite read his thoughts, his subtle facial expressions give him away. I know GI Joe can't tell, but Jarrod's scared. I am, too.

He nods his chiseled chin in my direction. "You're hurt," he says, as he positions his massive body in front of the open door.

I shake my head in confusion. "No. I'm fine."

"Your ear," he says and points the barrel of the rifle to the side of my head.

I reach up to touch my ear and pull back a bloody palm. "Scratched it when I was hiding in some bushes," I lie. An icy wave rattles my stomach. I have no clue why my ear is bleeding, or if the blood is coming from the inside or outside of it.

"Sorry," he says with no effect in his voice. "You guys are gonna have to go. We can't take anyone else in. Especially the Altered."

"But it's going to get dark soon," Jarrod pleads with an unconvincing fake tone.

The military man is silent. He stares us down, waiting for us to make a move—off the steps, or at him. I sense he's waiting for us to rush him. Something inside him is actually begging us to come at him, to try to take him down. He's looking for a reason to raise his rifle and put one right between my eyes. Or maybe he wants to alter Jarrod's scar by blowing a hole in the side of his face. But this stand-off has only piqued my curiosity more. Now I need to know what's going on inside there. I have to know what's up with the men on the roof. My existence cannot continue without the knowledge of the Southold Safe Zone's secrets.

Such stupid games I play with myself. I've been human, Infected, Altered, and changed again and *still* can't get over my obsessive-compulsive tendencies! But my gut told me. My gut told me that getting to a Safe Zone would get me information and help. Getting to a Safe Zone would put me one step closer to I-95. And it's right here in front of me—behind GI Joe, and behind those white metal doors.

I bend at the knees and pick up the green pack with all the medicine in it: Tylenol, Percocet, Xanax, Benadryl, Oxycodone, Lexapro, Fioricet, Robaxin, Jardiance ... there was bottle after bottle, and I just took it all. Just in case. That old lady had quite the stash in her medicine cabinet, which leads me to believe she wasn't alone in that apartment. I toss it over at the feet of the armed guard. "How about a cache of meds? Will this buy us two days?"

He lowers his weapon and cranes his neck closer to see the medicine. "Wait right here." He picks up the bag, goes into the school, and shuts the heavy door behind him.

Jarrod shoves me in my arm, and I almost lose my balance. "What, are you crazy?" he snarls through gritted teeth. "That's our stuff!"

"It's fine," I say with a side grin, "we're just going to let him hold on to it until we're ready to go. Did you see the way he looked at the bottles? They must be low on pills. They must be really desperate. And we gave him our only gun. Now they'll have no reason to fear us."

The door flings open, and GI Joe lurks in the threshold. This time, his rifle is strapped around his shoulder. After patting us down, he jerks his head to the side, signaling for us to come in. "Two days. That's all you can stay."

"Thank you, that's all we'll need. I'm Griffin, and this is Jarrod."

GI Joe doesn't offer his name. He closes the door behind us when we enter, and another military man, who is standing by a row of lockers, nods at him, grips his gun, and walks to the front door to keep watch.

The lobby at the entrance has a black-and-white checkered linoleum floor, and it is dark and cold. Not just physically dark and cold, but there's an unsettled silence throughout the building. Considering he said the place was packed, it has an empty aura to it. We walk down the main corridor, and I notice many of the lockers lined up in rows have been hastily pried open, as if someone tried to get into them in a hurry. From what I can tell, the opened ones are empty. Jarrod's head turns from side to side, and I know he too is drinking in all the details of this place.

"There are bathrooms on every floor," GI Joe says as he guides us through the school, pointing at all the important and generic landmarks. "Meals are served in the cafeteria down that hallway. A bell will ring for meals. Town hall meetings happen in the auditorium over there. And down that hallway, toward the back of the school, you'll find the gym. We use that as our rec room. Some like to play basketball, or run laps, but mostly we like to keep things quiet in here. Here's the stairwell. All living quarters are on the second floor."

"Who runs this place?" Jarrod asks as we walk up the stairs.

"We're military-directed," he answers flatly.

"So, the government is still in control?" I say.

He doesn't answer.

"The CDC? WHO? They must be working to fix this again, right?" I interject.

GI Joe huffs. "That's all classified information. I'm not at liberty to say."

"Who gives you orders, then?" Jarrod asks. "Marines? Army? Navy?"

Military man ignores his line of questions and leads us to classroom 202. "Here you go," he says as he opens the door and walks away.

It's a regular classroom with an old school chalkboard. It looks like a schedule is scribbled across the board in yellow and white chalk. Big check marks are etched beside some bullet points of a list, and deep X's cross out some other points. There's more of that linoleum flooring, too; only it's beige up here. The walls are painted beige to match, as well. The old wooden windows are closed tight to keep out the cold, and the wooden desks are stacked up and put along one of the walls to create a giant open space in the middle of the room. I quickly assess the area: a pile of old newspapers on one of the desks, blankets, pillows, sleeping bags, a laundry basket filled with clothes, and the gem of the room—a straight-line view to the parking lot from the windows. There are four other people; I guess they're the permanent residents of this space.

I tilt my head upward and inhale their scent—fear, anxiety, wonder: all three mixed together smell like rabbit stew with heaping chunks of boiled potatoes and carrots. It's warm and salty and hangs heavy in the room. My stomach twitches...

An older man and woman sit at the teacher desk playing cards while a younger woman reads a book under a blanket on the floor and a young boy with headphones on rocks back and forth to the music in his head. They all stop and stare at us when we walk in. The older man stands up in alarm. He extends his fingers on the desktop to give himself the appearance of extra height. He certainly doesn't need it though; he stands at about 6'5". A questioning and suspicious look comes over his face. The boy pulls off the headphones. The young woman peers up cautiously from her book. I look at

Jarrod, and he rolls his eyes, a gesture he most definitely picked up from me.

"Hi," I say, with a quick and nervous hand wave.

My voice echoes in this hollow room. "Hello?" the old man questions.

I point my fist to my chest and then to Jarrod's forearm, like Tarzan introducing himself to Jane for the first time. "I'm Griffin; this is Jarrod." My voice sounds so stupid out loud, and my ears get hot.

"What are you doing *here*?" the old man barks. "This is our room!"

Again, my senses go red in alert. This situation can go sideways real fast if I don't handle it with a little finesse, and I sense Jarrod's fury starting to rise again. He opens his mouth to answer, but I'm quick and stop him before he can say anything. "We're only staying a few days. We're just passing through. Looking for some supplies and some information, mostly."

The older man looks down at the woman at the desk, and they exchange a pained look.

"Why did they let you in?" he asks.

"We had something to trade," Jarrod says with a snarky tone.

"Trade?"

"We had some leftover medicine and a few weapons. The military guy at the door was pretty receptive to—"

The teenage boy sits up at attention. "You have medicine?" he eagerly blurts.

"Bradley!" the older woman scolds in a motherly way.

I give a little smirk. "Had." I look over to the tall man, Bradley's father I presume. "Like I said, we'll be gone soon."

His face tightens at the mouth. "That's highly unlikely," he mutters as he sits back down. I don't think he meant for me to hear his comment, though. "Listen," he says, "you two stay to one side of the room, okay? We don't want any trouble. My family will stay out of your way, and you guys stay out of ours."

I nod and unravel one of my sleeping bags packed with clothes and lay down. "We can do that."

Jarrod takes my cue and does the same. "And just for the record," he announces loudly, "Griffin and I are Altered. We were cured after the first outbreak. And contrary to popular belief, we're harmless. We're not gonna try to hurt anyone or any kinda funny stuff or nothing."

The older woman makes a croaking, gasping sound in her throat, and the other woman just stares at Jarrod. I tug on the cuff of his jeans to try to get him to stop. He looks down at me and winks. For a second, I see Josh's face, not Jarrod's, and I smile.

The boy shoots up from his spot in the room and scrambles over to us. He can't be more than thirteen years old. His brown eyes are filled with such curiosity and wonder that I know what he's going to say before he says it. "You ... you're *Altered*?" he asks, mesmerized.

Jarrod points to his scar. "USA Government-approved!" he brags in a non-bragging way. "Griffin is too."

"Yep." I point to mine.

"What happened to you? What's it like? Did you kill people? Did you eat people? Are you infected now? Can you infect me?" he rambles with his rapid-fire questions.

"Bradley James!" the mother scolds again. Bradley looks at her and sulks.

"Oh, it's okay, ma'am," I assure her. "A lot of people have a lot of questions. We're used to it. Actually, I don't mind it. I'd be curious, too, if I was him. I actually appreciate it more when people confront me with questions instead of just staring at me like a monster."

She sulks down in her chair with embarrassment, and I look at Bradley. "What were you, like nine years old during the first outbreak?"

He nods his head. His tufts of brown hair bounce wildly up and down over his face.

"How'd you manage to survive all that?" I whisper to him.

"We stayed in our house. Me, my mom, my dad, and my sister. We had a basement."

I smile but bite at the inside of my lower lip. They rode it out the first time. Most people who survived did. I didn't. Look what that got me. Look where that got me—in some worn-down school in New York of all places with a strange family and a psychotic companion. If I had just stayed in that house for two more days, even two more months, things now might be entirely different.

"What kind of medicine did you give them?" he asks.

"Just some Tylenol, painkillers, and some anti-depressants," I respond.

He looks over at his sister sheepishly. "And you're just going to let them keep all of it?"

I put my finger against my closed lips and shake my head "no." "Yes," I say loudly. "Every last bottle."

Bradley smiles; so does his sister.

"So where are you going after here?" Bradley asks.

"Florida," Jarrod declares. "Got some important business down there."

I pause and look to Bradley's father at the desk. "We're going to Florida to try to find my cousin. We were hoping that some of the military people could help us out— maybe give us some info or head us in the right direction."

"Give us a vehicle," Jarrod adds.

Bradley's father's face darkens. "The military? Military don't mean shit anymore. Haven't you heard? Or have you been hiding under a rock the past few months?"

Well, when you put it that way. Not under a rock, more like on experiment island...

"Actually," Jarrod starts to say, but I smack him on the leg.

Bradley gets up, walks over to the stack of newspapers, digs for one, and hands it to his father.

"This was one of the last printed papers from early October," the father says, as he holds it up.

The headline, in black-and-white print, reads:

Election Postponed Indefinitely as White House Goes Dark.

"THEY'RE DEAD! THEY'RE DEAD! THEY'RE all dead!"

My head spins. My eyes shift in and out of focus. Voices behind me scream frantically, sobs and gasps fill the air, and I want to comfort them, tell them to calm down, that everything will be okay, but I can't acknowledge it or respond. I can barely open my mouth to push out words. "Go," I manage to squeak. "Go."

Jarrod doesn't hear me.

"Oh God! Lilly! What are we gonna do now? What are we gonna...?"

"I don't know, Bradley! I don't know!"

I try to swivel my head to look at them in the backseat, but the second I move even a fraction of an inch, the ringing in my ears intensifies to a blinding crescendo. Jarrod's hands shake as he rips out the yellow and red wires from the steering column. It looks like a swirling bowl of spaghetti oozing from a brown canister.

"Go," I croak against the ripping feeling in my throat.

"I'm trying, I'm trying," he answers in a calm voice. A soothing voice. A comforting voice. A safe voice. One that I would like to listen to for the rest of my days and...

"No! No! We can't leave! We can't go!"

More screams from behind jar me from my safe place. But there are other screams, too. In the distance. In the building. On the roof. Men and women screaming all over the world, crying out in terror and agony, all at once, all at once...

"Bradley! Mom is dead! And Dad..." Lilly gasps and makes a strange hiccupping noise in her throat. "Dad ... Dad ... Dad..." She stutters like a record skipping on an old-time Victrola. It sounds kind of pretty, the way her voice lilts up with notes of tears. *Dad ... skip... Dad ... skip.* A nursery rhyme almost. My brain sets a musical track behind the skipping word, and I think I'm smiling at my new song.

I promise, Lilly, I'll remember this song forever.

"I'm not leaving without them!" Bradley screeches, dragging me away from my intoxicating melody.

Out of the car windshield, I see a group of people approaching from the darkness, coming across the back parking lot. Some move quick. Some move slowly. Some look as if they glide across the worn-down grass. It's a sweet dance they do, and for the life of me, I swear, some of them are singing an old familiar song. Not the "Dad" song that I've already forgotten (sorry, Lilly), but something more haunting, more guttural, more *natural.*

Lilly shrieks a blood-curling scream, and her pointed arm darts from the backseat in between Jarrod and me. "Oh God! They're coming!"

It's okay, I want to say. *They can't hurt me.* Even still, something deep inside my very being rattles with an urgency to flee this place, so all I can say is, "Go."

The engine comes to life, and Jarrod cheers. "We're in business, folks!" He puts the car in reverse, and we start to roll backward toward the front of the school and Oaklawn Avenue.

Gunfire pops all around us like fireworks on the Fourth of July.

"Go!"

Bradley squirms and wiggles. His feet jerk the back of my seat. "We have to go back for Dad!"

"Stop it! They'll kill you if you go back in there. *Dad* will kill you!"

"No! He won't! He'll be fine! He won't hurt me! I'm his son!"

The gunfire gets louder. The Infected get closer. I wave at them. There are so many, it almost seems magical. They swarm and appear out of thin air, like they materialized out of the shadows. They must have wizard powers or something. I think I smile again.

Bye, bye. My friends and I are going on a road trip.

"Bradley, it doesn't work that way, and you know it! You saw what Mom did to him! You saw ... look at that," she points out the window again. "They're everywhere. That horde will get you before you could even make it back into the building."

"I'm not going anywhere without Dad, Lilly! You can't make me!"

They struggle. I think Lilly tries to restrain her little brother.

I rub my temples with my sticky fingers, trying to rub my thoughts straight, trying to rub my focus back into something real and tangible. The sense of urgency bubbles up to my eyes, removing the thin veil of haziness that made me think absurd thoughts. I was injured in the chaos before, but something else happened to me— something curious that shifted my reality and made me feel ... *weird.* I grip my side of the dashboard and sit up. "How are we on gas, Jarrod?" I say with clarity, as he spins the car around and shifts it into drive.

He maneuvers the car down the rest of the long driveway like a pilot gliding an airplane in the open skies, turns right onto Oaklawn Avenue, and peels away from the school. "Full tank, Griff," he answers.

"Good. Let that full tank take us as far as it will."

"Roger that!"

"Stop! Please! Don't..." Bradley yells.

"Bradley," I say firmly, trying to calm him down. "It's going to be okay. It's all going to be okay." But even as I say those words, I know it's not. I look in the rearview mirror, and the Infected spill out from the sides of the school—from the parking lot, from the school itself, even from the depths of the cemetery across the street. Most likely, things are not going to be okay. Most likely, Lilly and Bradley are going to suffer terribly in this hell of a world and die miserable deaths like their parents and Lilly's husband did.

Before Lilly can add on to my words of affirmation, the lock on the back door clicks open. The air pressure in the car drastically shifts when Bradley opens his door and rolls out onto the pavement. Lilly screams his name, and in the rearview, I watch him tumble like a bale of hay.

"Quick! Shut the door!" Jarrod commands.

Lilly reaches over and pulls it shut. "No! Bradley! No!" she sobs.

"He's gone, Lilly. He's gone," I try to console her, but it's no use. The horde surrounds him, swallows him up, descends upon him, and clamors to get their hands and teeth into him. They quickly fade into the distance, and the image of them transforms into a giant gray blob before it fades out of sight in the darkness. "Don't look back," I say to her. "Faster," I say to Jarrod.

Lilly curls into the fetal position in the back seat as Jarrod accelerates. The engine's roar rattles the entire car, and I put my head back on the headrest to try and process the chaos that had quickly unfolded.

"What the hell was *that*?" Jarrod speaks my thoughts, and I know he's trying to process it, too. He's covered in blood from head to toe; even the socks in his sneakers are saturated with it—they're pink and make a squishing sound every time he presses on the gas pedal.

"Insanity," I say matter-of-factly.

"It all happened so fast."

"It felt like a dream, too," I interject.

His eyes widen like he's having an epiphany, like what I said resonated deeply with him. "Yes! Exactly! That's exactly how I felt! Like it was a dream or something. But you were *in* the dream, man. You were out of reality!"

"I don't know. I don't know. I just *felt* out of it."

"No man, it was more than just that. It was like you were sped up but moving in slow motion at the same time. Then you slowed down mentally but moved quickly." He pauses. "Almost like you were..." He stops and glances at me from the side of his eyes. Memories of that feeling shock me. Memories of having been turned and changed and turned and changed and...

Don't say it. Don't say it. I know what he's going to say, and I don't want him to say it.

"Did you bite anyone?" he asks, and I'm so grateful he didn't say *the* word. I could kiss him for not saying "infected."

"No."

He inhales deeply, and his bloodied shirt rises as his chest inflates with air. He bit people. He bit a lot of people.

And here we are...

"We came to the Safe Zone looking for answers, Griffin. I think it's safe to say things didn't go exactly as planned."

"Agreed," I answer, but his observation about my actions still bothers me. I replay the last few hours over in my mind, trying to make sense of it all...

●

Meals at the Safe Zone were held in two shifts because there were too many people to have them sitting in the cafeteria at once. At nightfall, the dinner bell rang for the first shift, and Jarrod and I went to eat with our roommates, the Bradford family. There were mostly humans in the dining hall, but I spotted a few Altered in the bunch. I nodded at a table of them as a sign of acknowledgment of our kind, like when strangers driving the same car on the road waved at each other or throw up the peace sign because they had some "vehicular connection." Curiously, I was ignored by my own people.

Better yet, I had thought. *They're not like me, anyway. Not really.* And it had dawned on me that maybe they knew I was different. Maybe they sensed that I was more Altered than Altered.

Dinner was relatively quiet and relatively atrocious. Ya know when people throw out that old idiom, "the tension in the air was so thick, you could cut it with a knife," and you're all like, "What the hell does that mean?" Well, *this* is what it meant. I could feel it like a heavy blanket on my chest. It was a suffocating feeling. As for the "atrocious" part, well, let's just say the meal was less than stellar. The military men in charge ran the kitchen just how you'd expect them to. Organized. Orderly. Efficiently. Bring your bowl to the counter, and GI Fred ladles out some concoction of stew. Stew-like substance? Stew-substitute? Stew-something. It was obvious that provisions were getting low.

Jarrod dipped his spoon in his bowl and pulled it out with a twisted expression. "What is this slop?" he bellowed. "They serve this all the time?"

John Bradford, the dad, leaned in close from the opposite side of the table. "It wasn't always like this," he said in a hushed voice. "The soldiers were pretty good to everyone at first, but with so many people to take care of, supplies dwindled quickly. They had to start making runs into town, and when their people didn't come back, well, things got a little…"

"Tense?" I suggested.

John nodded tersely. "When they lost contact with their stationed superiors, they started asking for volunteers to go with them on runs. And soon, we set up schedules where everyone was pitching in and taking care of the Zone. The guards we have now were the only ones left to run this place."

Bradley mimicked Jarrod and held up his spoon with disgust. "I like the days when Mom cooks in the kitchen. She cooks really good."

Mary Bradford, the mom, smiled.

"During the last run, Lilly's husband didn't make it back," John continued. "He was military, too."

Lilly hung her head down, her eyes focused on her bowl of mush.

"I'm so sorry to hear that," I said. But I wasn't. I didn't know him. How could I feel sorry about someone I had never met before?

"It's okay," she mumbled, and I knew she was holding back tears. She was around my age, and I thought it was kinda weird that she had been married. "One of the other guys said they saw him walking around the church the other day, but I'm too freaked out to even look out the window. I don't want to see him like that. I want to remember him being normal."

"So, they go on runs, you say?" Jarrod interrupted. "There are cars around?"

"Oh yeah, for sure!" Bradley exclaimed. "A whole parking lot full of them out back."

I looked at John. "What do you think the chances are they would give us one?"

He huffed out his nose, his nostrils flaring out like a mean dragon. "Slim to none."

"Not even after we gave them all our medicine?"

Lilly let out a soft sigh, and I noticed for the first time that her eyes were rimmed with dark, heavy bags and were sunken in. She was tired. Drained. Sad. But there was something else I couldn't quite put my finger on. Sick, for sure. If she wasn't, she wouldn't have perked up at the talk of the drugs.

After dinner, we went to the gymnasium for some rec-time. John had explained that the back-up generator used to run the building was only on for two hours a night, and those two hours covered the two meal and recreation shifts. After that, it was back to the rooms with candles and flashlights. In the gym, I had fully expected to see drugged- up Altereds in white hospital gowns aimlessly walking around or being pushed in wheelchairs by snippy nurses, like I did when I was in the Re-Assimilation Center. But it wasn't that way at all. It was your typical high school gym, with the bleachers pulled out and the basketball hoops extended down on each side of the court. There were some people shooting baskets, a few running around the perimeter of the gym at a steady pace, and some kids playing jump rope in the corner of the room. Lilly and Mary sat in the bleachers while Bradley tried to get his dad, Jarrod, and me involved in the current basketball game.

"Come on, Griffin," he said to me, but I waved my hand in the air and shook my head.

My attention had been captivated by the perfect view of the parking lot. The *car-filled* parking lot. Even in the darkness, my Altered eyes managed to scope out quite a few vehicles that looked perfect for my plan.

"Later," I said, and he scrambled off. John and Jarrod joined Bradley on the court, and I walked over to the window and gazed. The wheels in my head began to turn, and I envisioned myself walking through the back doors with Jarrod, getting into one of the many cars in the lot, and driving off into the night. But reality never plays out that way. Things always work out more perfectly in my visions. I think that's true for everyone. But it seriously would have been so easy, too, if that GI guard wasn't positioned near the back door. With a suspicious eye, he watched me surveying the parking lot. He watched me as I strolled from window to window, calculating my escape route. I knew he knew what I was doing, but I didn't care. I was busy figuring out the hows, whens, and whys of my plan. Actually, I don't think he had a clue what I was planning.

"What are you gonna do about it, asshole?" I vaguely heard someone yelling on the court. I was so deep in thought that I wasn't paying attention to the argument that was brewing. It was Jarrod, of course, because Jarrod was always mouthing off, always had something to say.

When we were on Plum Island, his mouth had nearly gotten him killed. I swear, I think Dr. Rennard tortured his poor sister even more as sort of a payback for Jarrod's outbursts.

"Come on, you freak of nature!" an angry voice shouted. "Let's go right now!"

Before I could even figure out what the hell was happening, the echoes of screams filled the gym, and the guard raced past me and into the fray. Jarrod and some other guy were tangled up on the floor punching away at each other, with Jarrod easily getting the best of him.

Quickly, I ran over to the fight and pulled Bradley aside. "Go upstairs with your sister and get all your stuff!" I commanded. He looked scared and confused but did as he was told.

GI guard pulled Jarrod off the man and punched him in the stomach. Jarrod let out a *poomph* sound and seemed to double over in mid-air. The guard then dragged Jarrod across the hallway and into the principal's office. It was pretty clear this was Jarrod's plan all along.

And this is when the dream kicked in.

Mary's head swiveled side to side with great panic. "Where are the kids? Where are the kids?" she repeated over and over.

"They went upstairs," I said, but I don't think she heard me because she wouldn't shut up about it.

More guards had come into the gym to make sure the situation was defused. The guy that Jarrod had been wailing on stood up and was yelling at them. "Who the hell is he? You let him in and compromise everything we've worked for? I'll beat the holy shit out of him. Let me have him." He was out of control, and I was becoming more anxious as our escape plan started to unfold.

I breathed a sigh of relief when Bradley and Lilly raced back into the gym with their stuff.

But that guy just wouldn't stop. When the guards finally let him go, he made a mad dash for the principal's office. The door slammed. I stayed at the back of the gym by the back door with Lilly and Bradley. My hands started to sweat, and a chill swept over my body. An iron-like smell filled my nose, and I arched my neck to try to locate the source. My senses piqued and dulled at the same time. My ears filled with fluid as if I were underwater and...

Then the screams began.

Slashing sounds and tearing sounds and groaning sounds and biting sounds and bullet sounds. The gym erupted in chaos, and I stood in front of the kids, putting my arms in front of them, as if to shield them from the nightmare unfolding.

The poor Bradford parents, overwhelmed by the confusion, stood frozen in their places. The door to the office flew open, and Jarrod came charging across the hall and into the gymnasium, covered in blood, green pack in hand. He seemed to glide across the slick surface of the gym floor and nearly knocked us over.

"Go!" he screamed at me and tossed me the bag of meds. His voice sounded a million miles away, and when he yelled, he spit blood into the air. It sprayed my face, and I extended my tongue to catch a taste of it.

And the taste left me swooning, hazy, drunk.

Just a taste...

Jarrod tried to get the back door open, but his hands were so saturated with blood, they kept slipping on the handle. Then there were more screams.

Look! I thought happily to myself. *Friends have joined the party!*

The newly infected guard and the asshole Jarrod had beaten up raced out of the office and into the gym.

There was blood everywhere. There were slashing sounds and tearing sounds and groaning sounds and biting sounds and bullet sounds—a dissonant melody that made me stop and soak it all in.

Bradley shook my shoulders and told me to hurry up, but I pointed into the gymnasium. I had something to show him. I pointed at the frozen John Bradford. I pointed at the infected Mary Bradford jumping into the arms of John Bradford and ripping the flesh from his face with her teeth.

The world got a little blurrier after that, and I faintly heard Jarrod say "Go!" again.

And I don't recall how I got in this car.

JARROD DOES ALL THE DRIVING WHILE I DO the navigating, and Lilly curls up in the back seat, moaning and sobbing, occasionally calling out for her parents, or brother, or for someone named Tim, whom I assume is the husband that was infected at the Safe Zone. Sometimes she giggles to herself—brief moments of hysteria sweep over her, and she can't seem to control or contain the emotions. What is she to us, and how did we come to drag her along? I know Jarrod's distaste for people would have let her and her brother stay to turn into Infected at the Safe Zone. But one night as we drove aimlessly around, she said, "We used to vacation in South Carolina. I can take us to the interstate. The 295 will get us there." That is about the extent of her contribution to the mission at hand.

Once we get to I-95, our use for her will expire. If Jarrod wants to toss her down the highway, I don't think I will be able to stop him.

The interstate is desolate, and it looks nothing like those post-apocalyptic scenes you see in the movies, either. In those films, there are usually abandoned cars littering the lanes of traffic so that the hero and his band of companions have to maneuver carefully around each and every car. The tension is high because they cruise so slowly, and the audience is just waiting for the zombie horde to descend upon them. This is nothing like that at all. We're doing ninety mph on the open road for as far as the eye can see. We passed a car zooming on the north side of the highway about twenty minutes ago, but that was it. Smooth sailing. It's exactly like I thought—everyone stayed put. Everyone is holding tight for a rescue or relocated to some shady Safe Zone (that may or may not actually be safe). As long as we stick to I-95, we're golden. With minimal stops along the way, we should make it to Tampa in less than a day.

I make Jarrod stop the car and pull over to the right-hand lane as we cross over the Throgs Neck Bridge. The sun breaks over the horizon, and the sky gleams with that melted pink-and-gold color. He fights me on it at first, but eventually gives in. I roll down the window and let the cool morning air fill the car. Lilly breathes it in happily behind me, and I poke my head out of the window's ledge, taking it all in. Normally, the busy bridge would be noisily bustling along, and a sunrise like this would be caught in the corner of the drivers' eyes as nothing but an afterthought or maybe even a clock of sorts. But now, against the stillness of the city below and the desolation of the once-busy highway, the sunrise is massive and all-consuming. It's a focal point—a reminder to us that we are simply just a small part of this world, and when the Infected eat the humans and the humans kill off what's left of each other, that sunrise will still show up every morning until that sun burns itself out.

"You hear that?" I ask Jarrod.

He shrugs his shoulders. "Hear what?"

"Silence. No cars, no trucks, no buildings coming to life with people waking up. Just quiet."

He closes his eyes for a second, his brain inhaling the sweet sound of nothing. "Yeah. I guess you're right."

I continue to stare out at the vast wasteland of a city—a city that is now frozen in time, paralyzed with disease, stricken with abandonment. A blast of mid-autumn air presses against the side of the car unobstructed. My head snaps back a bit at the bite of the stinging breeze in my face, but when I return my head to the ledge of my windowsill, something in the distance stirs. A rumbling echo rises from the depths of the city below us, and I pause my thoughts to tune in my senses. The din jangles at first like Jacob Marley's chains in the afterlife, and I can't pinpoint exactly what it is I'm hearing. Jarrod's head perks up, and I know he's tuned in, too. It rises, slowly in accordance with the rising sun, and its volume increases slowly but surely. Until my ears eventually discern the elements of the cacophony.

Symphony.

The infected wail, and screech, and *sing*. And over their dissonant chorus, another sound rises up above the concrete jungle trees and buildings, carried up on the morning air like prayers to the heavens above.

"No! Please! Don't!"

Something in the song resonates deep within me—fills my mind, heart, and soul with an insane sense of longing, regret, guilt, empathy, and serenity all wrapped up in one. The song touches me in a way that I can't describe because I still have much to wrestle with inside myself. Who am I? Who have I become? I thought I knew at some point along the way—thought I had a moment of clarity back when I had set out to help dead Dr. Holston take care of his Altered, but now? Not so much. These last few months have left me so foggy, I have no idea whether I'm coming or going. I have no idea who I am or where I belong.

The song rises up louder, and Jarrod and I look at each other. With a nod of his head, and without saying a word, he starts the car again, revs the engine, and continues over the bridge.

The three of us are silent the rest of the way until we reach I-95. I've almost forgotten about Lilly in the back seat. She cried herself to sleep and has been out cold since we crossed over the Throgs Neck. On the one hand, I feel sorry for her—everything in her world disintegrated so quickly, she's probably having a hard time processing all of it. But on the other hand, I know I can't allow myself to feel any sort of attachment to her. She's only going to slow me down. I wonder when we get to Tampa if Dr. Graves wouldn't mind helping her out. I bet he could Psych 101 her real good!

Oh, Dr. Graves! I wonder what state this second outbreak has left you in.

"What happened to you back there?" Jarrod asks, ripping me from my thoughts of Graves.

"On the bridge?" I ask.

Jarrod looks at me out of the corner of his eye and raises one eyebrow. I always wished I could do that. "No!" he says, raising his voice. "At the Safe Zone."

I shrug my shoulders. "I dunno. I'm not sure. I know you pretty much infected the entire Zone."

He snickers. "Yeah. It was like dominos, man. I think I only bit two or three of them, and it took off from there. It happened so fast."

I nod. "You're so bloody," I say absentmindedly. And then I remember tasting blood and swooning into a stupor.

Jarrod laughs again. "Good observation, Griffin. You are, too."

I look down at my shirt for the first time and see that yes, I am indeed a bloody mess. The front of my shirt is splattered with blood like a child's painting. But still, I feel uneasy. "Blood sprayed everywhere, it was..."

"Amazing."

"Horrifying."

"You sure you didn't bite anyone? You were acting kinda..."

I think about it for a second and cut him off. I don't want him to say the word. *Don't say the word, don't say the word.* "I'm pretty sure I didn't." I rub my temples and scrape at the dried blood with my dirty fingernails. "I don't know. We both acted ... *strangely* ... which is even more reason why we need to get to Dr. Oswald. If her lab is up and running, maybe she can tell us what's going on with us."

I sense Lilly tense up in the back seat. She's awake. She's heard our conversation.

"We've been back for a while now, right?" Jarrod says, and it's more of a statement than a question.

"You mean 'away from Experiment Island'?"

He nods.

"A few weeks." I pause, anticipating his next statement. "Why? What's up? What's going on?"

He hesitates. Stammers a little. "I ... I don't know. I can't explain it. Sometimes I just feel..."

"Different?"

He shrugs his shoulders. "Yeah. Maybe. Could be. I ... I don't know! Do you know what I mean?"

We haven't had the drug that Trager had been giving us in a while, and the thought crosses my mind that we might be going through some kind of withdrawal. I don't mention to him the growing pangs in my stomach, or my cravings, cause they're not really there; they're not really there; they're not really... "I think so. Different how?"

Jarrod closes his eyes and inhales, trying to gather the right word to pinpoint the feeling that's been creeping up inside him. He doesn't need to speak it out loud because the word comes to me at almost the exact same moment.

Hungry.

"Hungry," he finally says, and hearing it rings true.

Hungry.

I hadn't noticed it, but the word makes so much sense to me now, and I guess I can't deny it any longer. It was *always* there, slowly working its way in the pit of my stomach, slowly moving up my chest cavity. I ignored it and ignored it, and pushed it down, but when the word hit my ears, there was no denying the pink elephant in the room anymore. As a human, as a stupid, unenlightened human, I was hungry. Young men love to eat, and I was no exception. When I was infected, I suppressed my hunger for as long as I could until the infection took hold of me, and I had no other choice but to give in to the cravings.

Then, I was cured, Altered. And the sight and smell of food was unappealing. I ate for the preservation of my semi-human self—it was the Altered way, as all Altereds spoke about this peculiar side effect of the antidote. Then I was captured and imprisoned and experimented on with Trager's injections, which suppressed my appetite even further and did God knows what to me. Then my escape. Cold turkey. And now. It's back. My stomach has growled quite a few times these last few weeks, I just chose not to acknowledge it.

Lilly shifts in the back seat, and I smell her scent waft in the car—her movement stirs up the smell of baked bread with a lemon glaze coating of pure terror. Jarrod and I glance at each other and give each other a "look." I know he smells her, and I wonder if it smells the same for him or if it's different. What scents does he associate her with? Is she savory? Sweet? Rancid? He scrunches up his nose and shakes his head quickly, signaling to me that he's not too keen on her aroma.

I look to the backseat and outstretch my arm to touch her. Her face is buried in her hands, and she's whispering something to herself. A mantra of protection? A prayer? She's startled when she feels my hand upon her knee.

"Lilly," I say in a gentle voice, "it's going to be okay. We're going to get help. We'll be safe in Florida." Part of that is a lie.

"I won't be safe with you though, will I?" she says through her fingers.

"You will, I promise," I coax, and it hits me that I have such a soft spot for broken girls. Her fragility and helplessness shines in her swollen eyes. They are round and dark blue like the depths of the ocean and are filled halfway with tears on the precipice of spilling over and onto her cheeks. "Jarrod and I aren't going to hurt you. We couldn't. We can't. You helped us. You're with us for the long-haul now." I lie again and squeeze her knee to reassure her.

Her body relaxes, and she drops her hands from her face. She sniffles once more and blinks her eyes rapidly.

"Okay," she says breathlessly and reaches between her legs. "Okay," she says again and pulls out Matt's gun and lays it in her lap, and I pull back my hand. "Just stop at the next rest area. I have to pee."

I nudge Jarrod's leg, and he looks at Lilly in the rear-view mirror. "We're not gonna do anything stupid, are we?" he says.

Her eyes spill out their tears. "Nah," she half-sobs. "We're cool. I just ... I just don't feel good."

She's scared. *D'uh*. Who wouldn't be? I know her fear. I know her uncertainty. And I know her fear for the uncertain path that lies before her. I guess it doesn't help that she got dragged along with two unsavory characters like Jarrod and me. And even though that fear smells delightful, I have no real intention of doing any harm to her but am completely convinced that my time with her can't last all the way to Florida. One loose cannon is enough. Somehow, we'll have to part ways before I reach my destination.

"No worries. We'll find something to drink at the next rest stop. We'll go through the medicine bag to see if there's anything you can take to make you feel better." I give her a soft smile, and she manages one back.

The rest stop in Maryland is deserted. Jarrod pulls up close to the convenience store, and the three of us get out. Jarrod walks around to my side of the car, puts one hand on Lilly's shoulder and extends the other, palm out.

"Give me the gun," he commands. "I know how to shoot it, and I'm willing to bet you don't. If anything happens out here..."

She looks down at the gun, then up at me and Jarrod. Terror is written all over her face, and her hands shake as she reluctantly hands it over to him. I actually feel better knowing he has it.

The glass window in the front of the store is busted in, and it's obvious the place is picked clean. Lilly heads straight for the restrooms, while Jarrod and I sift through the aisles, searching for anything useful.

"Not much," I call out to him, but honestly, there isn't anything by way of food that Jarrod or I want—or crave. I grab a few items for Lilly and shove them in one of the packs.

Lilly comes out of the bathroom and wipes her hands down her legs. "I was thinking..." she starts to say, but Jarrod jumps up from his crouched position and runs to her side. He grabs her by the hands and drags her to the floor. I freeze in my tracks and listen to the sound of another car pulling up into the parking lot of the rest stop. Jarrod clicks the hammer on the gun, readying it for use, and I inch my way to them quietly.

Lilly cranes her head up to see what's going on. "An RV," she reports. "Looks like a family. A woman got out. She's testing the gas pumps."

"Is she getting anything from them?" I ask.

"Looks like it." Her voice hitches in her throat. "Oh no! Big man. Coming this way."

Just like she said, a large man comes into the store, tripping over some of the debris on the floor. Jarrod automatically pops up and trains the gun on our intruder. "Back up, big guy!" he threatens.

The man stops in his tracks and puts his hands in the air. "We... we don't want any trouble," he squeaks. "We're just looking for supplies."

Jarrod takes a step forward, crunching through the fallen potato chip bags. "I said to get the hell out!"

"Okay, okay!" the man says, backing up out of the store.

The three of us advance, following him outside. I immediately go to our car to make sure our stuff is still in there.

The man's wife gasps when she sees a gun pointed at her husband. "Oh please!" she begs. "We just needed some gas and some medicine. One of our sons is sick. We're trying to get him help."

I look to the RV, and pressed against the three windows on the side of the vehicle are the faces of three little boys. One of them has his pale cheek mashed on the glass. His big black eyes are sunken into his face, and he looks ghostly—ghastly. Lilly grabs my hand when she notices him, and he stares at us with those vacant eyes.

"Was he bitten?" Lilly asks the woman.

"No! No! Nothing like that."

Jarrod keeps his aim on the man and walks to a gas pump to fill our car.

"Sir," the man says, "we don't want any trouble."

"Neither do we," Jarrod answers. "I'm gonna fill our car, and we'll be on our way. Then you can do whatever you need to do and go wherever you need to go. Just don't make a move until I say so."

The man nods at him. "Is there any chance you all have some kind of medicine to help my boy?"

Lilly nudges my arm.

"No," I lie. "There's Tylenol and other over-the-counter stuff inside that you can take."

The man shakes his head. "No. I think he needs antibiotics."

"Nope, sorry," I repeat, but Lilly nudges me again, giving away my deception.

The woman picks up on this and runs over to me. "Please!" she begs in my face. "Please! Anything. He has a fever. He won't eat. There has to be an infection in his body. Please! If you have anything to help him..."

I take a step back to create some distance and look up at her sickly child in the RV. He's pathetic-looking, like death is one footstep away from reaching out his hand and whisking the little boy away. He's weak and can barely keep his sunken-in eyes open. They shut, then open, shut, open—the black color rhythmically flashing on and off.

Until they open again and aren't black anymore.

I freeze when I see the boy's eyes have hazed over white with infection. His hand reaches up and lazily slaps at the window, and I know his body is slowly but surely adjusting to its new feelings. I tighten my grip on Lilly's hand and calmly whisper out the side of my mouth, "Get back to the car, now."

She listens, and I turn on my heels to follow close behind her. The woman takes a step to follow me and yells another "Please!" before screams erupt in the RV. I look over my shoulder, and the window with the sickly child is empty. The window where another little boy was is now splattered with blood stains.

The woman turns around and begins to scream. The man takes off for the RV, yelling his sons' names. I put my hand on Lilly's back and quickly usher her into the car. Jarrod caps the gas tank and hops back into the driver's seat.

"What the?" he yells in disbelief.

He plops the handgun in my lap and starts the car.

The RV shakes from side to side, and I can only imagine the struggle taking place within. Jarrod steps on the gas pedal, and we race back onto I-95.

"**T**HIS IS EXACTLY WHAT I'M TALKING about!" Jarrod rants over the roar of the engine. "This is exactly what I mean about not being able to trust people!"

Lilly cries softly in the backseat like a child. She tries so hard to stifle her sobs so she can look strong and tough, but I can hear right through it. I know there's a little bit of fight left inside of her somewhere deep down. I mean, hell, she had a lot of nerve pulling that gun on me! I understand why she did it. I know she wouldn't really ever be able to use it. It reminds me of my mother and her idle threats about eating our lunch or cleaning our room and how she was going to "give us a fresh one" if we didn't obey. I never knew what she meant by that...

"We had that run-in with those people at the café. Look how that turned out!" he continues. "We get to the creepy Safe Zone. No explanation needed there. Now we have spontaneous infected family at the rest stop! People are dangerous, guys. That's the bottom freakin' line."

Lilly sighs. "But that family wasn't going to hurt us. They needed our help."

"You don't know that. That woman lied to us. Her kid must have been bitten in order to have turned. And she said he wasn't. She lied. Why did she lie? Because she was up to no good."

"We don't know that for sure," I interject.

Jarrod pauses and gives me a scowling glance. "Like I said, bottom line is we can't trust people."

"But I'm trusting you guys," Lilly croaks pathetically, and the sound in her voice lets me know she's on the verge of a major crying outburst.

"We're not people," he says matter-of-factly, and Lilly slumps further down into the seat.

"At least, not in the sense of how you know people to be," I say.

Jarrod glares at me again and looks at Lilly through the rearview mirror. "Let me tell you something," he begins. "My sister, Margo, and I … after we were Altered and our lives started to get back on track again, we hooked up with these humans. They were fascinated with the Altered. Wanted to be like us. Wanted to know what it was like to live our lives. It was fun for a while, but it was ultimately a dead-end. Got Margo killed. Left us nowhere."

"Now and here," I mumble.

"But, you took me with you. I'm a human," Lilly says. "Doesn't that mean you trust me?"

"No," Jarrod replies. "It don't mean shit."

He's right, and I wonder again why the hell we're keeping her around. The heat of the moment, the rush of the chaos. She just kinda got swept up in our journey, and she really has no business being with us. I'm not interested in being tied down to another person. It's bad enough I have to contend with Jarrod, but he at least has proven himself useful. Lilly doesn't seem to add much to the equation. I look in the side mirror, and her face is contorted like she's been punched in the stomach, so I end the conversation by turning on the radio.

Static shoots out of the speakers from every FM station on the dial, but I remember something from a science class I once took about how AM radio waves work differently from FM. If someone out there is broadcasting in the immediate area, we'd be able to pick up a signal.

Static. Static. More static. One station plays Spanish music, but I'm guessing that's been pre-programmed on some kind of loop. I fiddle with the dial trying to get the right balance of sound and static from one of the stations when we hear a faint voice come through.

"Hey! Listen to this!" I exclaim.

Lilly scoots up from the back and leans her head in between the bucket seats.

"...*Hermitage High School on Hungary Spring Road in Richmond. We have food, shelter, running water, and protection. Hermitage is outfitted with personnel from all branches of the US military. All are welcome to...*"

"Bullshit!" Jarrod roars. "That's totally fake!"

The transmission pauses for a few seconds then restarts. "*Safe Zone 363 is open for refugees. Hermitage High School on Hungary Spring Road...*"

"How do you know it's fake?" Lilly asks.

"Safe Zones were voluntary holding places. Matt said that people in each area only had forty-eight hours to get to one, or else they had to fend for themselves."

"He's right," I add. "They're probably luring people looking for help. Leading them right into an ambush."

"Well, maybe no one stopped the loop. Maybe no one stopped the transmission after the forty-eight hours."

Her innocent naivety is half-charming and half-vomit-inducing. "I highly doubt it," I say.

"Again! Don't trust the humans." Jarrod bangs his hands on the steering wheel, and I turn the radio dial.

"*...the end of days. Infection will get us all in the end. What is left of this Earth will be the new age of mankind. A new era. A new dawn. We will rise from the bloody mess and...*"

Religious fanatics. Nothing like a good plague to bring out the most holy.

I try one last time to see if there's anything else out there—anything meaningful, helpful; hell, I'll even turn back to that Spanish music station again!

"Go back!" Lilly says. "Turn back a little. I thought I heard someone laughing."

"*...so yeah, that's been my day so far. Seems like the same thing every day, doesn't it?*"

It's a female voice. The transmission is faint and choppy, but we can definitely make out what she's saying. And the one thing that I do register is that this broadcast is live. On an AM station. Short wave. It's possible she's in the vicinity!

"Jarrod, slow down a little. I don't want to lose this feed."

"*...and yeah well, could you imagine if this is what my channel consisted of? The fine people of YouTube would have thumbs-downed me into the grave.*" Her laughter ends with a sorrowful sigh. "*I doubt anyone is listening, but for all my newcomers, welcome.*"

Funny how she addresses us, but I bet she says that every day. She has a professional sound to her voice, and I wonder what kind of internet channel she had back in the day. Makeup tutorials? Politics? Current events?

Sports? Fashion? Toy reviews? The transmission cuts out for a few seconds, and my heart stops thinking we lost her.

"...fresh bites are always fun. That's good content, I suppose. Would be even cooler if they actually did something to me. So yeah, dear people of the infected world, no show here. Sorry, but if that's what you paid to see, you got gypped."

"She's Altered," I say out loud. That was meant to be an inside thought, though.

"Wait? This is happening right now?" Jarrod asks surprised.

I nod. "She must have some pretty decent equipment."

He leans over to turn up the volume. Static hisses as the broadcast briefly goes offline.

"...just wanted to feel something again. I know that sounds so stupid when I say it, but at the time it made sense in my head... Cathy used it ... bit me ... nothing happened and ... Altered immune to the bites. I thought we'd go back to our normal Altered lives after we used Black Death, but Cathy," she sighs again. *"She couldn't stop, so that was that. Infected her whole damn family, who then infected the whole damn neighborhood, who then infected the whole damn city, then the whole state, then the whole country, then the whole world."* She laughs in spite of herself. *"Now, I know that's not* exactly *what went down, but if I had to gamble, I'd say that was probably the same scenario in most places..."*

"She's all alone," Lilly says to no one in particular.

"... payback, I suppose. Payback for all the horrible things I did the first time around. Things that were beyond my control ... no one's coming ... I'd be a fool to think otherwise ... when I was infected... surviving..."

"I feel bad for her," Lilly says.

"Why?" Jarrod asks. "Because she's Altered? Because she's alone? Because she watched her best friend overdosed and killed everyone they knew?"

Lilly pulls back a little and hesitates. "Well, yeah."

"I don't, and you shouldn't either," he barks back.

Jarrod's right. This radio broadcast, this confessional, it's all anchored in deep-seated guilt. She's a performer, and she's performing. She talked about "This is her payback" for the sympathy vote, but in all actuality, she's okay with her current situation. She's made peace with it.

"If she wanted help, she would have asked for it," I say.

"But she did ... in a way ... kinda..." Lilly stammers.

I shake my head. "If she did, she would have given her location. She would have repeated it over and over and over all day long."

"Aleksander from Denmark ... the timeline we pieced together with all our charts and shit. Day One. Terrorists, or so they would have us believe ... six months in the deep trenches soaked in blood and ... released the virus in the big cities and that's all it took... slow acting... the infected people boarded planes, went to malls, attended schools, and boom—the slow build materialized to something... quick and violent..."

The transmission stops, replaced with white noise.

"Still makes me wonder where she is," Lilly says.

I won't deny her that—the broadcaster's location has crossed my mind a few times.

"...then some crazy fuck goes and makes Zombaxin! Why? Cause people just couldn't get enough? Aleksander said they crushed the pills in the hash bars of Amsterdam and smoked it in their joints and pipes ... one night ... could you imagine? The whole hash bar turned from the

contact high? That must have been crazy!" She chuckles again and pauses. *"Ya know what's even crazier? My mom ... running around outside ... dead chicken in her hands ... trying to get into the house ... must smell me, but ... when they drop the nukes..."*

Lilly reaches over the seat and shuts the radio off. Her arm brushes up against mine, and her baked-bread smell catches my nostrils. I close my eyes and breathe in the scent—the glorious scent! I want to comfort her, but then again, I want to push her out of the moving car. But then again, I want to bite through her throat, yank her trachea out, and gnaw on it like a doggy chew toy. *I won't eat it, I promise. I just want to play.* These are the emotions that shape me now—the human side of me feels sympathy, the Altered side of me feels anger and rage, the Infected side of me feels ... *hunger*. All the different versions of me are in a never-ending battle, fighting for my soul, and tearing me apart from the inside. I shake my head violently, trying to shake away the thoughts from my brain.

She purses her lips tightly before saying what's on her mind. "That kid from the RV? He had to have been bitten, right?"

"Logically speaking?" I answer. "Yes. But who knows? This infection has evolved so much, there's no telling what's happening with it."

Her fingernails dig into the back of my seat in a shear rush of panic. "Why? Do you think it's airborne? Will I get infected? Will my baby..."

"Baby?" Jarrod bellows before I get a chance to respond.

"You're pregnant?"

She lowers her head and lets her mass of brown hair cover her face. "Yes. Maybe. I don't know. I can't be sure yet. Too soon to tell. I think," she stammers. "I haven't been feeling well, and..."

Jarrod and I look at each other wide-eyed. This new revelation changes everything, and for some strange reason, a feeling of protectiveness comes over me. Like, I need to do for Lilly what I couldn't do for Crystal. I need to protect them. Get them to Dr. Oswald. Oswald will know what to do. And who knows? Maybe Lilly and her unborn child can be useful in stopping this outbreak. I had no reason to care about her before, but this is a whole different story.

She twirls her hair around her forefinger. "Do you think we could stop somewhere for the night so I can...?"

"No!" Jarrod says without hesitation.

This time, I agree with Jarrod because I'm focused on getting to Tampa as soon as possible. Spending the night somewhere will slow us down. "We'll get off at the next rest stop to use the bathroom and stretch our legs, but that's it. Jarrod, I'll drive next."

Jarrod looks at her in the rearview. "The Richmond stop is a few miles off. Do you want to go there, or wait for the one after?"

"Get off in Richmond," she says, defeated.

Jarrod veers off the exit when it comes up. The drive from the Infected RV in Maryland to Richmond was about three hours total, and the sun is already starting to shift in the sky. The time on the car clock reads 4:00 p.m., but time has become such a strange concept to me that I scarcely notice it. I can judge time by the position of the sun and the change in the air pressure. When you're Altered like me, little things like that just tend to come naturally.

Ya know what else comes naturally? My gut instinct. Coming to a stop right as dusk rolls in doesn't feel like the right thing to do. When I step out of the car, there's a slight hum in the air that I can't quite put my finger on. It's heavy, like humidity weighing down on your chest; only this is in the back of my ears, and it gives them the sensation of being filled with water. The feeling puts me on high alert, and I motion to Jarrod. The expression on my face must be a dead giveaway because his senses are on high alert, too. That's the one thing he and I have in common—Altered perception.

Lilly and Jarrod get out of the car. Jarrod tests all the gas pumps, and Lilly says, "I'm going to the restroom."

I fetch the handgun from the front seat and assertively tell her, "Just hurry up. It'll be getting dark soon, and we should be on the road."

She smells like bananas as she glides passed me.

The wind picks up, and a shot of cold air blasts me in my face. On the breeze, I pick up multiple scents—infected smells, people smells, burning smells, blood smells. The last one is so strong, it's intoxicating, and my stomach dips with excited hunger. I could easily slip into a drunken swoon right now, but a humming noise in the distance nags me too much. What is it? Where is it coming from? I scan the perimeter of the rest stop and see we're surrounded by a thick woodland area. *Anything could be lurking out there*, and cold dread washes over me. I whistle to Jarrod, and he looks up from the pump. I wave the gun in the direction of the treeline. He nods in agreement and puts up his forefinger, signaling "one more minute" to me.

When I was real little, I was afraid of my closet. Not necessarily the dark, but my actual closet. To my child eyes, it stretched deep and wide to a never-ending alternate world. At night, crazy things came out of it. But crazy creatures came out of it during the day, too. Whenever I played in my room, the door to the closet always had to be closed, and at night, my father tied his belt around the door handles to reassure me nothing was coming through. When that closet door was open, I swear I could feel eyes staring right at me—eyes that beckoned me to enter, implored me to navigate its creepy depths, waiting for me to step inside and snatch me away from my parents forever.

I tighten my grip on the gun, and Jarrod trots back over to the car. "Let's go, Griff."

"Where's Lilly?" I ask. Jarrod's face goes white.

I swivel my body to see Lilly being pulled by her hair by a man dressed head to toe in black. He points a gun to her head. I point my gun at the man and prepare myself to take a shot, but Jarrod calls my name, and I turn to see he, too, has a gun trained on him.

"Put the gun down, and they won't get hurt," the voice grumbles behind the black ski mask. "Put the gun on the ground and take two steps back." The words sound stupid, like one of those mystery robbery-type movies. "Lower your weapon!" "No one has to die today!" "Step away from the gun, sir." Dumb words. Cliché. Couldn't anyone think of anything better to say?

I don't say a word and do as I'm told. Lilly and her assailant get closer and of course, she's hysterically crying.

"We're taking your car and anything else you got," he says, shoving Jarrod into the side of the car.

I look around the parking lot and notice something I hadn't noticed before—there are no other vehicles around. The place is completely desolate. If they take our car and our supplies, I have no idea what we'll end up doing.

"Take what you want," I say gently. "We have some food and medicine, but please, don't take the car. We need it."

"So do we," he says.

"No, you don't understand..."

"You don't understand. We're gonna take the supplies and the car, and if you don't shut up, I'll blow that girl's head off."

Lilly hides her face with her hair like a little kid playing hide and seek under a blanket. Does she think she disappears under there? Does she think we can't see her when she hides like that? Jarrod bucks against his captor, and I give him a stern look.

"Please," I say, grasping at straws. "You really don't understand. My sister," I look over at Lilly with a mock loving expression, "she's pregnant. We need the car to help keep her safe."

Jarrod's captor lowers his weapon. "Oh. You hear that?" he says to the other guy.

Lilly's captor picks my gun off the ground and points it at me. "Altered," he sneers. "Move!"

I step to the side, and he shoves Lilly into the back seat. The other guy shoves Jarrod to the ground and fires his gun next to his ear. I rush over to him to see if he's okay, and the two assailants drive away into the wooded area with Lilly ... and our car.

AFTER RANTING AND RAVING FOR A GOOD fifteen minutes, Jarrod finally settled down. We ran through all the questions: the what-ifs, the whys, the hows, everything. Who were they? Why did they take Lilly and leave us behind? Why didn't they just kill us? And most importantly—where did they go, and how can we get the car back?

"We probably can track them into the woods," I say.

"Oh yeah? Cause what? You're some kind of tracker and hunter?" he scoffs.

"Actually, car tracks aren't really difficult to follow. They took the car down that way." I point to the wooded area across from the gas station.

"Look, I don't think we should risk it..."

My mouth drops. "Don't think we should risk it? What are you talking about? After everything we've been through? After all the crazy shit we've seen and done? *Now* you're saying don't risk it?"

"This is for that girl, isn't it?"

My heart stops, and I swallow hard. "No! Not at all!" I lie.

He raises an eyebrow. "So, you're saying we should trek through the woods to steal back a car we already stole from people with guns and who knows what else. Griffin, it's just a car. We'll get another one."

I can't leave her. I need to convince him that we need to go after them. "Oh yeah? Where from, Jarrod? Look around. I don't see anything. No people, no cars. Do you see anything? We could be walking for days just to find another one."

"So, we walk for days!"

"That's not the point!"

"Then what is the point, Griffin? Explain it to me."

I'm hazy. Fuzzy. At war with myself. Saying these things out loud really does make my whole wanting to track down strange men with guns in the woods sound stupid. I want to explain it to him. I want to explain the song I have in my soul for Lilly, but I just can't find the words, and...

"Admit it. It's about that girl. You want to play hero. You want to save her."

"No. No. Really. I don't. I swear." Lies. Lies. More lies.

He snickers. "It's okay if you do. I mean, if you're into the sickly type."

My eyes shift focus. The world spins around him. I can't catch my breath. "Stop it. It's not like that. It's just that I'm..."

"Chicks are kinda hot when they're infected, too. They get all wild and white-eyed, and they try to lash out at you!"

I put my hands over my ears to block out the sound of his voice. "It's not her! I'm just... just..."

His face screws up, and he points at me. "You're just bleeding again! Jesus, Griffin! What the hell is wrong with your ear?"

I am? I hadn't realized. I look at my hand, and it's smeared with blood. The iron smell reaches my nose, and my stomach growls fiercely. I exhale. My lungs deflate and I find my center, so the world stops spinning. I am clear— focused—able to pinpoint my motivation for wanting to go after them.

It's not just for Lilly, either. It's not really for revenge. Hell, at this point, it's not even for the car. "I'm just ... so *hungry*."

A surprised smile sweeps across Jarrod's face. That was all the explanation he needed. "Well, when you put it that way."

The last specks of daylight filter through the tree canopy as we come upon a perimeter fence in the middle of a clearing in the woods. A red farmhouse with a white wooden wrap-around porch sits regally in the center of the field. To the left of the house is a barn with rickety doors. A couple of tool sheds are next to the barn. There are about six or seven people milling about the land with shovels and spades in hand. We stay hidden within the shadows of the outlying trees—a trick we've gotten pretty good at. Tire tracks lead from the gates of the fence, curve over the land in front of the farmhouse, and lead to the barn. That's where our car is, I know it.

Jarrod nudges me and points to the front porch. Lilly sits on a wooden swing. A woman in a pink flannel nightgown with short brown hair sits next to her and rocks them both with the balls of her feet. Lilly has her arms wrapped around her waist, and she's doubled over as if in pain. The woman pets her back in a loving way.

"I told her not to trust people," Jarrod mutters.

"But *she's* a human. I think your advice fell on deaf ears."

"Looks like they're being nice to her, at least."

I'm shocked that he would even comment on something like that. I bet he's having the same war on the inside like I'm having.

"C'mon," I say, motioning for us to move closer.

"What's the plan, boss?" he whispers as we stealthily navigate through the brush.

We've become hunters on a mission—hunters stalking their prey. My stomach gives a low rumble, and the people smells linger in the night air. "I don't know. What do you think?"

"Well, that depends on how hungry you are."

Hunger is a feeling I struggle with. It shakes me to think that I'm giving in, that I'm out in the woods *hunting* people—to kill and eat. I'm caving in to the cravings. I'm seduced by the anticipation of the swoon. I long for the high of that feeling that sends me over the edge in ecstasy. *I'm chasing the dragon, Frankie Z.* No Black Death watered-down version, either. This is the real deal. *I am* the real deal. A voice inside me reminds me to make sure they're dead, or else they'll end up infected.

But wait.

Why does that matter? Why would I care? The world's not coming out of this nightmare, so why wouldn't I just do what I need to do and walk away?

My hands are slick with sweat, and we watch the people going in and out of the farmhouse. One by one, a potential meal comes into my sight, and I breathe deeply to steady my anticipation.

"Do you think we can take the whole compound?" Jarrod whispers.

"Hmmm ... not at once. We'll have to..."

Something rustles in the woods behind us. Ambles. Shuffles. The trees sway in the distance in a ragged motion. It's too far away for the people to notice, but Jarrod and I do. There are Infected approaching, and he and I need to decide real soon how we're going to descend upon the group.

"Listen," I say and turn my head to the conversation on the porch.

The two men who stole our car and took Lilly walk up to the woman on the swing. They hold shovels in one hand and flashlights in the other. "You let the two Altered men go?" she asks them.

"Yeah," one of them answers.

"You should have brought them back here with you. I might have been able to use them."

Jarrod chuckles quietly. "We *are* here!"

I can't contain a small laugh, either.

"If not for that, then for our general protection," she continues, her voice rising in anger. "How many times do I have to tell you about outsiders? When are you guys gonna get it? You remember what happened when..."

"But then they said she was..." one of the guys jumps in.

The woman stands up and raises her hand to silence him. "Thank you," she says and smiles. She reaches out her hand for Lilly to stand up next to her. "How far along are you, Lilly?"

Lilly slumps her shoulders forward and shrugs. "I'm not sure."

The woman holds the side of Lilly's face with her hand and wipes away the tears with her long thumb. "It's okay. I'll help you figure everything out," she coos, but Lilly grimaces and tries to back up when the woman presses her long thumbnail deep into the side of her upper cheek—just underneath her right eye. Lilly lets out a squeal of pain, and a thin line of red rolls down her cheek. "Oh!" the woman exclaims with a false tone of concern. "I didn't mean to scratch you! I'm so sorry. I'll take you upstairs and get that cleaned up." And she wraps her arms around Lilly's shoulder and pulls her in close to her chest.

Jarrod mumbles "What the hell?" under his breath, and I swat his thigh to shut him up.

"Did you get the barrel out?" the woman says to the guys. "Heading out now," one replies.

"Good. And the Metro Zoo?"

"Overrun. That's when we lost the car. The first car. We'll go back tomorrow," the other says.

"Okay. I'm taking the girl upstairs. Come get me when the barrel is out."

The two nod and trot away, and the woman ushers Lilly into the farmhouse. If she is taking her upstairs, she should be safe from the approaching horde. Once the horde passes through, I'll be able to run in and get her. But only after I...

The rustling in the distance gets a little closer. "I think we should move," I whisper.

Jarrod tilts his head to the side and listens with his preternatural hearing. His face narrows as if he's heard something that I didn't pick up on. He pulls at my shirt and leads me around through the trees to the back of the farmhouse. "Do you think we attract them?" he asks when we can no longer hear the distant noises.

I think about that for a second. A long time ago, my crazy old Aunt Marianna had told me she wore men's cologne. When I asked her why, she responded with, "Men are attracted to their own smells," and proceeded to tell me how the young men in the neighborhood always helped her with her groceries and held doors for her when she was wearing men's cologne, but on the days she wore her lady perfume, they all but ignored her. At the time I laughed it off and was tempted to tell her that young men do nice things for old ladies. But perhaps there was something valid in Aunt Marianna's theory.

"It's possible," I whisper back. "Maybe they can smell how we're the same as them and they want to 'check us out.'"

"Or maybe they smell how we're different, and they're curious about us."

I shrug my shoulders. Quite honestly, I don't care. I just want to make my move and indulge in the most gruesome way I know how.

The two men with shovels come into sight by the side of the house and begin digging through the grass and dirt. We duck down to our knees and peer out from among the bramble.

"What the hell are they digging for?" I say, but when one of the shovels hits something underground with a metallic clang, Jarrod's eyes go wide, and he tugs excitedly on my shirt sleeve.

"Oh my God, Griffin! Let's go!" Jarrod mouths breathlessly. I know he doesn't mean "go," as in "Let's get out of here,." He means "go," as in "Let's make our move. Strike. Attack. Bite. Chew. Feed."

As much as the urgency swells in my stomach, a wave of panic snaps me back to the situation at hand. I shake my head.

We stare out as the two men heave a steel drum up and out of the earth. It's industrial- looking—stainless steel, about fifty-five gallons. They pull and grunt and struggle to get the barrel out and upright. Whatever is inside, it is heavy, or it's jam-packed with items.

This time, I grab Jarrod by the sleeve and lead us further away from the house and deeper into the woods, out of earshot or eyesight.

"What's up? What's going on?" he asks.

I shake my head again. "If we're doing this, like really doing this, we need a solid plan."

"Wait, why? There's like ten people in there. I was able to singlehandedly decimate the Safe Zone. Put us together, and this will be a breeze."

My ears go red, and my cheeks get hot. The human side of me screams "Shame!" on the inside for even thinking about this plan. The Altered side of me screams "Hooray! Bout time you stopped pussying about and got revenge." The Infected side of me makes my stomach roar.

"These aren't just a group of people banding together haphazardly to wait out the apocalypse, Jarrod. They're Preppers."

"What does that mean?"

"Preppers. They've been prepping for this probably since the first outbreak. I've seen documentaries about how they live—it's very cultish and downright strange. They stockpile their homes with canned goods; they freeze-dry meats and even whole-prepared meals; they hoard bottled water by the gross. It's insane what they do! That barrel they dug up? Well, they probably have hundreds of them buried all over the property. What they do is fill each drum with as much stuff as possible, then they go out at night and bury them fifty feet apart from each other. But it's all secretive and shit. Only four or five people in the group know where the barrels are buried. It's like a weirdo treasure hunt or something."

"Okay, so they thought ahead. Good for them. What does that have to do with us?"

"Compounds as big as these can hold up to thirty people, maybe more. Who knows what's in that barn, in those sheds, and even in the farmhouse basement."

Jarrod wrings his hands together. My reserved nature doesn't mesh well with his "guns-blazing" instincts.

"And...?"

"And ... they have weapons. Lots of them. A full arsenal, in fact—probably even more than those military guys at the Safe Zone."

"So, what are you saying, Griffin?"

"I'm saying, let's be rational about this. We may be immune to infection, but we're not immune to bullet holes."

"So, then what?" He pleads like a child not getting his way.

"I don't know. Let me think about it."

But I got nothing. I should have just walked off the nearest exit on I-95 and found myself another car. I should have just pushed my hunger to the side like I've been doing and stuck to the original plan. I should have taken that gun and shot both Lilly and Jarrod in the face when I had the chance. Should-a's. Could-a's. Would- a's. Doesn't erase the fact that I'm Now and Here. *Nowhere.*

Not human. Not Altered. Not Infected. *No one.* I pace back and forth, and the crackling noise in the distance returns. The sound of it suddenly jumpstarts my brain into motion—the wheel turns, and the conveyor belt of my genius mind goes round and round and round.

"They're coming, ya know."

Jarrod flails his arm in the air. "I know. I know. I hear 'em."

"Why don't we sit back and see what happens?"

"They could take all night to get here, though."

"So, let's kick back. Snoop around a little. Wait for our cousins to show up and cause a little commotion..."

Cause Lord knows they don't scare me, but guns do...

Confusion grips Jarrod's face. "Instead of fighting them, join them?"

I nonchalantly shrug my shoulders. "Sure, why not?"

Jarrod's smile returns, and his dark eyes brighten. "I like the way you're thinking, sir. Like a true war machine. Good strategy. Infiltrate from the inside."

"We'll have something to eat, get the car back, and return to original Plan A."

"Okay, okay, I'll bite."

I lower my eyes at him sternly. "Not yet."

Jarrod laughs. "True, true! Not yet!"

E HAVE THE COVER OF DARKNESS ON OUR side as we prowl around the outskirts of the perimeter gate. Someone screams from the farmhouse. From the timbre of the yell, and the high-pitched tone of the voice, I know it's Lilly. A second round of screams permeates the woods, but this time, they are quickly stifled. Gagged. And I wonder if Lilly's light of life has been snuffed out.

For a team of Preppers, they sure did a pretty lack-luster job of securing the back part of the fortress. Jarrod and I are the only ones back here bumbling around in the brush. Behind us, in the distance, I sense the horde coming. I feel the vibrations in the ground rattling my nerve endings; I hear the moans faintly carried on the breeze. I close my eyes and tune into their movements and from the shift in ambience and buzzing and smells and tension, I get the notion that there's a lot of them. Maybe too many for this Prepper group. I'm not sure what their arsenal looks like, or how their defenses will hold up, but if this horde is as massive as my senses alert me, these Preppers are in for one hell of a fight. Regardless, we have some time to kill before they make their grand appearance, so Jarrod and I slowly make our way to the barn. I know the car is in there, and when everything goes down, we will have the car in our sights, and after our Thanksgiving Day feast, we can get the hell out of there.

"I've always been this way," Jarrod confesses. "Since I was first turned. It never stopped. It stopped for Margo when we were Altered, but not for me."

"What never stopped?"

"The hunger. The rage."

"That's why Trager wanted you, I guess. Something about you aligned with his vision."

A branch snaps beneath Jarrod, and he mumbles a string of curses under his breath. "Why you? What did Trager want with you?"

I can't tell him. I can't make the grand confession of my own and reveal that I'm the prototype child of the Altered OG, Dr. Holston. I can't tell him about my time at the Re-Assimilation Center, or about Graves, or about the treatment and help I received even after the center was shut down. There's no telling how intense Jarrod's hunger and rage would grow if I did. "Dunno," I lie. "Could have been he wanted info on the boy."

"Troy? Nah. There's was more to it. He saw something in you. You're definitely more reserved than I am."

"So, maybe he wanted the perfect killing team? The Yin and Yang of the Infected world."

Jarrod shrugs his shoulders. I think I said enough to placate his curiosity. Unless his Altered senses are far more superior than mine, and he saw right through my line of bullshit. I doubt that, though...

The door to the barn is loosely secured with a two by four, and it's opened wide enough for us to slide our bodies right through the crack. At each corner in the room, there is a stake stuck in the ground that holds a plastic lantern. The lanterns glow with soft LED lights, and the barn is partially illuminated. The bottom part of the barn is their garage, as there are six cars parked in rows.

"Take your pick!" Jarrod says in a hushed voice.

I spy the car we were in—the white Honda Accord. "No. We should just take back the one we had. We know it's gassed up, closest to the door, and you're familiar with the wires and all that. To hotwire another one would waste time, and we don't know if they're in working condition. Let's stick to what we know."

"Good point. I knew there was a reason I kept you around."

Wait. What? Keep *me* around? He's lucky I'm keeping *him* around. And then it dawns on me: maybe Jarrod is just as aggravated with me as I am with him. Maybe he knows I'm lying to him about what happened to me. Maybe he's waiting for his moment to kick me out of a moving vehicle. "Don't trust the humans," he said. But what about the Altered? What about Jarrod? I think it would be in my best interest to just not trust anyone.

Something stirs outside the barn, and the muffled voices of people manifest in the night. There are steps leading up to the loft, and we scramble up and out of sight. The lantern lights don't reach up there, so we're completely hidden. We lie down in a bed of hay and remain completely silent and still. Two women armed with shotguns shimmy through the doors and start opening the car doors, looking for something.

Are they looking for us? Were we spotted?

"Al and Ed said there's a group of them heading our way. Good thing they dug up that barrel, cause by the way Ed made it sound, we're gonna need all we got soon," the redhead says.

"Hmmm," the woman with the salt-and-pepper hair grunts. "Hey! Where did this Honda come from? Where's the Toyota?"

"They lost the Toyota at the zoo," the redhead says.

Salt-and-pepper slams a car door. "Sonuvabitch!"

The redhead laughs. "Al said there were too many Infected there. Guess they couldn't handle it. I told Heather that if she sent me and you, there wouldn't have been a problem."

Salt-and-pepper chuckles. "Yep. Al and Ed are good for nothing. I don't know why Heather trusts them the way she does. Did they at least get anything useful from the lab?"

"Some more tranqs. That was all Heather told me."

"Specimens?"

Red-hair takes out the red pack from the back seat of our Honda and places it on the hood. "What do you think? This is Al and Ed we're talking about!"

Salt-and-pepper laughs again. "No Infected and no animals."

"Seriously? At least get an Infected. Poor old Betty has seen better days!"

Red-hair puts her hands on her hips. "And they talk tough saying they're real men! Mind you, I've taken down at least five Infected by myself! Now, to be fair, I would imagine that Komodo dragons are pretty hard to wrangle."

"Oh, we could do it!" Salt-and-pepper interrupts.

"Damn straight we could!" Red-hair agrees empathically. "But I guess I can kinda see their point. Being surrounded by Infected and all."

"Oh please! Ed probably pissed his pants the second he heard moaning! Anything good over there?"

"Just this." Red-hair tosses our handgun over to Salt-and-pepper. "Yeah, I bet Heather wasn't too happy when they came back empty-handed. Tranqs are good for now, but she's looking for the big payday. She's been dying for that Komodo for forever."

"Heather hasn't been happy with much of anything lately."

"Rightfully so. Shit, if you lost your kids—"

"I know, I know," Red-hair interjects. "I can't even imagine." She tosses the red pack back into our car. "Come on, let's get ready to kill some Infected scum."

The two women leave the barn, and we rise from the hay, dusting off our pants and shirt sleeves.

"Whatever operation they got going on over here..." Jarrod begins as he moves toward the stairs, but his words are interrupted by a crash and a muttering of obscenities.

"You okay?" I ask.

"Yeah, yeah. I'm fine. Bumped into this trunk."

My curiosity always gets the better of me. I kneel down beside him and feel around in the dark for an opening on the trunk. The chest's lid creaks up, and inside are stacks of papers. "Jarrod, you still got that Maglite on you?"

He reaches into his pocket, takes out the flashlight, and shines it into the depths of the treasure chest. "What's all this?"

It doesn't take a genius to make sense of the papers—documents, questionnaires, newspaper clippings, medical records, forms. I'm familiar with some of the terminology found on some of the files from my experience with working with Dr. Holston's stuff at the Brandon Medical Center.

"Medical records, mostly. They were doing more here than just prepping, that's for sure!" I say.

Jarrod reaches in and pulls out a stack of papers. He skims through them before stopping at a hand-drawn diagram. "When the blood sample is injected directly into the placenta..." he reads. "Griffin, what the hell is this place?" He holds up the diagram and shines the light on it.

Outside, the moaning of the Infected swells like a lullaby being carried on the night air. It's louder now. Closer. Their song distracts me from Jarrod, and I inch over to the small window in the barn. In the not-so-distant woodlands, a mass of movement approaches against the starlit sky like a black wave rolling languidly upon the tree-filled shore.

"They're coming," I say, and Jarrod joins me at the window. "See." I point out at the black line of the horizon, only it isn't the horizon; it's the crowded bodies of the Infected moving in time. "They move together in the darkness. They're staying together."

"They know," Jarrod says. "Me and Margo always stayed together."

I've observed (and experienced being) Infected enough to understand that the day-to-day life is different for each individual. Infected had a bond with their kind but acted on their own. It was a weird pack-versus-individual mentality. When I was infected, I raced with the pack but hunted alone. It was like having company over for a few hours and then relaxing in solitude. Even before I turned, I watched them from the second story in my parents' house, and I don't ever remember massive herds plowing through the streets. I don't remember ever being a part of a herd. Just another reminder of how the game has changed.

Something stirs in the hay on the other side of the loft, and Jarrod and I look at each other suddenly. "Animal?" I suggest.

"This is a barn, right?" he agrees.

The hay moves some more, and a gurgling sound faintly rises up.

That curiosity of mine, I swear...

I tip-toe around the corner of the loft to where the noises are coming. Jarrod is right behind me, flashlight guiding my every cautious step. The rustling in the hay gets more animated as we approach, and suddenly, an arm reaches up from the pile like a zombie arm escaping from the grave. I pull back the long, yellow straw in clumps to uncover a woman in leather strips shackled to the floorboard. She's emaciated—the bones in her face jut out underneath her sunken-in eyes, and her lips curl up over her rotting teeth. Jarrod pans the flashlight over her body, revealing track marks and bruises up and down her pale, skinny arms. She's a bag of bones—a heap of *infected* bones.

"What the...?" Jarrod says, moving the light to her face.

She moans softly and rolls her white eyes into the back of her head, probably to avoid the brightness of the flashlight.

I take a step closer and kneel beside her. She's so weak, she can barely move, but with whatever strength and energy she has left, she chomps her teeth down in my direction. She can't even growl, and I think how sad it is for an animal to be without its voice. I touch her shoulder, and she squirms as much as she can stand. Her dirty shirt lifts to the side, exposing fresh rudimentary stitches across her abdomen.

"They're experimenting," I say. "They're experimenting on pregnant women."

"So that means..."

"Lilly," I finish for him. If Lilly is truly pregnant, I don't see how she is going to come out of this alive.

"Do you think they're looking for a cure?" Jarrod asks.

I stare at the Infected woman and smooth her hair from her forehead. She tries to chomp at me again, but I think it's just a natural reaction; I don't think she's trying to eat me. She's been a prisoner for who-knows-how-long, and instinct is probably all she has left. Her sad, white eyes lock on mine, and I wonder if she's in pain. Can she feel pain? I can't remember if I felt pain when I was infected. All I remember feeling was the need, the drive, the desire, the *hunger*. I ran through the ditches, scraped my fingernails against concrete until my hands were bloody, smashed my head against steel lampposts, and all that never hurt my body—never registered as sensory pain in my brain. But when the hunger grew too strong, the overwhelming ache throughout my body was agony.

"It's okay," I whisper to her, "it'll be okay." I lift up her head and cradle it in my hands.

Our brethren get closer. She senses them too, because she closes her eyes and sways slightly to the music of their song. The gentle motion of her body rocks her back and forth. I want to hum to her, sing to her, but I don't want to ruin what she perceives as a happy moment—the happiest moment she's probably had in a while—so I sway with her, rocking her back and forth. I think a small smile creeps up on the side of her mouth.

"God, Griffin! How can you touch it?" Jarrod scoffs.

Easily. I can touch her so easily and without hesitation. She's a part of me. Of the same blood, of the same substance, of the same disease pumping through our veins. She's seen horror, just as I have—experiments, tests, a slew of torturous trials performed on us like we were hunks of meat.

Suddenly her eyes shoot open, and before I know it, there's a commotion in the forest followed by echoing screams. I lay her head back gingerly in the hay and look at Jarrod. "They're here."

"Sounds like the Preppers aren't prepped," he jokes, and judging by the sounds of the scream-filled forest, I can't argue with him on that. "Let's go downstairs. Wait 'til the first wave hits."

A loud gurgle comes from his stomach, and I raise my eyebrows at him. "Think you'll be able to hold out?"

"Yeah, yeah," he says dismissively. "Let's go."

I get up on my knees and look at the Infected prisoner once more. "What about her? What should we do about her?"

"Her? Nothing! Are you serious right now?"

Yes. Serious. I would seriously feed you to her, only you're not the right flavor. "We can't just leave her."

"Whatever. Do what you want. I'll be down there by the cars."

He throws the flashlight at me and leaves the loft. I don't know what I can do for her, or how I can help her, but I want to make sure she's at least free when her brothers and sisters come barreling through. If she has the right idea, she'll ride the wave like me and Jarrod and be able to get some semblance of sustenance. I hope it's that Heather woman, too, because I'm pretty sure she was the one who locked her up.

They called you Betty.

I unbuckle the belts on her shackles and slip the thick leather off her wrists. She moans louder at me and gives one chomp. "You're not so scary, Betty. You're gonna have to work on your delivery. Gotta find your voice again." I lean over, sit her up, and stand next to her. Gunshots pop in the forest, and I jolt from the noise at first. Betty is unfazed. "Come on, let's go," I command her, but she doesn't move. "Come on, Betty; you're free now. Free to hunt. Free to be."

She still doesn't move. She can't. A pained expression sweeps over her mangled face, and she stares at me with her sorrowful white eyes and a gurgle in her throat.

Even the Infected have their breaking point.

Is it the pain from the starvation? Weakness from the fragile state her body is in? Trauma from her battery of testing? Is it the memory of the child that was taken from her and an unwillingness to satisfy her basic needs?

Just looking at her makes me angry. *That very well could have been me shackled to the barn beam.*

Just looking at her sparks my rage. *The curiosity of man knows no bounds.*

Just looking at her makes my stomach turn.

"Griffin, let's go! They just breached the gate!"

Just looking at her makes me wild with hunger.

Don't worry, Betty; tonight, I'll eat enough for the both of us.

J

ARROD POKES HIS HEAD THROUGH THE slats in the barn doors. "We gonna dance, or we gonna play? Your call, Griffin."

Dancing—I never liked it much. I think a lot of my disdain for the act was due to my two left feet. I couldn't keep a beat, either. You have to have rhythm, you have to have soul, and sadly, I was not blessed with either. It takes a certain person to be a good dancer—hell, it takes a certain person to just be able to *dance*. Never mind the "good" part, just the part where you get up and start moving your body to whatever music is playing—feeling it, grooving to it, letting something in the rhythm take root in that invisible part of you and drive your body to contort and constrict and ... dance. When I was a kid, the school would hold all kinds of dances. I went to one. *One*. I swear, I wanted to hide behind the gymnasium bleachers and never show my face again to the world after Josh had dragged me onto the dance floor and started shaking his body around me in a weird and quasi-perverse way. It was awkward and embarrassing, and every eye in that gym was trained on my stupid attempt at herky-jerky movements. But Josh didn't care; he never did. He was just *Josh*, and even though he wasn't a very good dancer, he still did it. He had the courage and carefree nature to just *be*.

Hunting people when I was Infected was a lot like dancing. When the hunger came over my body, and I no longer felt in control, I would let the primal instinct to feed sweep down and grab the invisible part of my soul and move me—drive me. It was like a beautiful choreographed ballet with pirouettes and dips and all that other ballet shit. I pranced and pounced and glided and soared. *And I was good at it.* Not just good out of necessity—I was masterful. Artful. *Soulful.* I moved with ease and grace to the rhythm of my heart and the whooshing sound of my blood pumping through my veins.

Like now.

I hear the music rise up within me, mixed with the moans of the Infected and the screams of the humans. It's enchanting.

Listen to them, the children of the night. What music they make!

Yes. I want to dance.

"Maybe I should stay by the car," I say.

Jarrod pulls back. "Wait! Are you backing out on me now?"

"No. Not backing out. Just rationalizing. Wouldn't it make sense to have the car ready to go and one of us close by just so it'll make it easier to get away? Like, if things go sideways real fast, like they did at the school?"

Jarrod scratches his nose. "The car does have a full tank of gas. And I do understand what you mean. I'll start her up and let her run while we take care of business, and she'll be all set when we need her."

He agreed with me without a fight? That's interesting. Jarrod starts the Honda while I guard the barn door. The first line of Infected come moseying through the back perimeter fence. There's enough of them to tear the chain-link down with their sheer weight, but there's no urgency in their actions, no real drive or desire in their approach because the open hail of gunfire mows them down. Their bodies collapse face forward onto the hard ground.

They weren't very good dancers.

I want to scream at them, grab them by their shoulders, and shake them into awareness. Watching their demise fuels my pain, my anger, my rage! It also gives way to the ultimate hunger.

Jarrod joins me at the door again. The car engine purrs, and at first I wonder if it will draw the attention of the humans in the compound, but that thought leaves my mind when I hear the shrieks of lamentation. The humans are far too busy with the onslaught of the Infected to worry about the Honda running in the barn.

A breeze blows through the doors, bringing with it a mixture of intermingling aromas—the sour smells of the Infected and the sweet, flavorful scents of the humans. A bouquet of rotted meat with undernotes of char-broiled steak tinged with a spray of misty blood. Now isn't that a dainty dish to set before Griffin King? Only this time, I'm in my countinghouse, counting all the dead bodies. Jarrod's counting, too—counting the seconds before he rushes into the fray.

I survey the scene. There are a lot of Infected wreaking havoc on the humans, a lot of humans holding their defenses, and a lot of weapons firing away. I look over to the farmhouse, and in the second-story window, the woman who brought Lilly inside is armed with a sniper rifle and aims at something in the forest. I catch a glimpse of Lilly's side profile. She's safe and secure in that upstairs room, which is a good thing. I will come for her when everything is clear.

"We can't do anything yet," I caution. "Look to the farmhouse. She'll snipe us if she sees us."

Jarrod huffs. "She don't know who we are!"

"Yeah. And that's why she'll shoot us."

Dummy.

Even with the first line decimated, the Infected continue to press forward like soldiers in an army. They're unstoppable. I can only imagine the insatiable hunger they must feel. No. Imagine isn't the right word. Rather, I *remember* clearly how it felt, and I empathize with them.

On the side of the farmhouse, a young man's gun jams, and his inability to shoot an Infected causes him to lose valuable time. Panic invades his face, and a line of sweat runs from his forehead and into his eyes as he fiddles and fidgets with the weapon. He dares not to wipe it away, for any second lost could mean his death. But he's too late. His panic-stricken hands are too shaky and slow, and the Infected is on him in a flash. The Infected knocks the man down on the front end of the porch and guts him with ease. Like giant spaghetti strands, he lifts up the man's intestines and passes it around to some of the other Infecteds around him. I've heard of family-style dining, but this takes the cake! When the young man finally stops screaming, I know he's *dead* dead. There's certainly no coming back from an evisceration, even if you tried. I tuck that into the back of my mind. I need to remember my cardinal rule from back in the day—don't change anyone.

Jarrod taps me on the shoulder. "Griffin, you're bleeding again."

"What? From my ear?" I reach up to the side of my head, and sure enough my earlobe is wet and sticky.

He moves in closer to inspect it. "What's going on with you, man?"

"I don't know. I didn't even feel it."

"Are you sure you weren't bitten?"

"Positive! Does it look like it's cut or something?"

He pulls at the top part of my ear and folds the ridged cartilage forward. "Not that I can see. I think it's bleeding from the inside."

"The inside? I…"

Jarrod leans in and licks the side of my neck. His long tongue slides up my collarbone and when he gets there, he takes my earlobe into his mouth and sucks on it. I jerk away from him. "What in the hell did you do that for?" I yell—agitated, disgusted, and creeped out all at once.

He puts up his hands defensively. "I just wanted to see!"

I frantically wipe his saliva from my neck. "Wanted to see what?"

"What it tasted like."

"Seriously? You can't wait until…"

Jarrod chuckles. "Sorry. Sorry. I couldn't help it."

"Well?"

He furrows his brow in displeasure.

"What did it taste like?"

"Like licking a rusty banister."

No wonder the Infected don't want to eat us. We Altered taste horrible to them—not like the yummy flavors of the humans with their fresh inside ingredients. I kinda feel bad that I taste bad. It kinda makes me want to know what Jarrod tastes like. Does he taste like me? Or is he different? That was always the beauty with humans—each one had their own distinct smell and flavor; it was like an open buffet of the most delectable fare.

"Good. I hope you choke on it. Don't ever do that again."

"Oh, trust me. I definitely won't!"

Shots ring out from the second-story window of the farmhouse, and my attention turns back to the second wave of Infected making their way to the field. This group is different than the first. This group runs and screeches and howls and lunges. Some are actually *lunging* at the humans. I've never seen them do that before! Suddenly, they're all over the place, as if they woke up or something. They swarm the farmhouse, and there's too many of them for the Preppers to keep up with. Some of the humans run away and abandon their posts. The farmhouse is now completely overrun, and the woman with the sniper rifle disappears from the window. A high-pitched screech rings out, and I hear someone tumbling down a large flight of stairs. Screams rise to a fever-pitch for a second, then subside to the low, dull moan of the Infected.

The song fills my ears again. Even my bloody one. Makes me sway. Makes me groove. Makes me want to get on the dance floor and show off my moves. My stomach is an empty elevator rising to the top of a high-rise pent-house. It stops at each level and opens its doors. My heart beats in time with the chaos in the field. *Thump-thump-thud-thud.* Closer and closer against my chest, I swear it will burst out and shower Jarrod with its irony flavor.

Just one ... just one ... just one ... just one...

"It's now or never, Griffin," Jarrod urges, but he doesn't need to tell me twice.

I nod sharply, and we push the barn door open and go running off into the fight.

Just one ... just one ... just one ... just one...

The field is littered with bodies—dead Infected, dead humans, and newly Infected waiting to wake up and greet the world with their brand-new set of whitened eyes. Some of them are already starting to change—the body twitches, the contorted shapes they make, the foam and black bile spewing from their mouths. An Infected lunges at me and takes a bite at my shoulder. She cuts me open with her teeth, and my blood rises up through my grey shirt. One taste of it sends her twirling on her heels and seeking out other prey. I never got the chance to tell her I'm a rusty banister.

Jarrod is gone. He went off howling and screeching to the farmhouse. I know what he's thinking, too—Infected can't climb stairs, so if there are any humans hiding out on the second floor, they are his for the taking. *Just don't get shot, you lunatic.* I don't want to stray too far from the car in the barn, though. There's a part of me that needs to remain cognizant and focused. Eye on the prize, ya know?

Humans and Infected whiz past me and stir up the air as they race back and forth. It brings with it one of my favorite smells—an all-American barbeque with every type of meat you can think of and all the trimmings. I close my eyes and inhale, savoring the sweet, sweet aroma from the gods.

Just one ... just one ... just one ... just one...

I look around trying to map out my best course of action when a vision of heavenly loveliness catches my attention. Red-hair stumbles down the porch steps of the farmhouse and walks out into the open field. She tears the rifle off from around her neck and tosses it to the ground. Her hands and the front of her camouflage shirt are blood-stained, and she staggers as if she were intoxicated. She's shaken up some but hasn't been bitten. I can tell because she smells like freshly baked chocolate chip cookies.

Just one … just one … just one … just one…

I rush up to her and catch her right as she's about to collapse. She folds up perfectly in my arms as I gently cradle her, hold her, caress her. There's a subtle warmth to her radiating from deep within, and I pull her closer to me to steal some of her heat. Her heart sings to mine when I press her chest closely to me.

"Karen," she mumbles weakly. "I couldn't…"

"Shhhh," I say, pressing a finger against her soft, bloody lips. "It's okay."

Tears spring to her eyes. "Please. Help me." A gurgle rises to her throat, and she coughs it out, spraying a fine line of misty blood into my face. "Oh, no! I'm so sorry! I'm…"

The scent hits my nostrils, and a chill of ecstasy quivers in my bones. I open my mouth and extend my tongue to the corner of my lip and get a hint of her pure, uninfected life force. Like candy. Pure sugar. Saccharine sweet. My head buzzes.

Just one … just one … just one … just one…

"It's okay. It's okay," I try to reassure her. "I got you now."

"But Karen. She's… she's…"

"She's gone now. We need to get to safety."

I don't want this moment to end or be interrupted by talk of her salt-and-pepper-haired friend. I want to hold her warm chest close to mine and have our hearts sing this sweet lullaby forever, but the mayhem around us is getting out of control, and I fear an Infected will try to snatch my beloved cookie princess away from me. But she's so wet—her bloodied shirt soaks through mine, leaving her scent all over me. It envelopes me completely. And she's so warm with fiery hair like a roaring fireplace on a cold winter night. She gives off just enough heat to make me feel toasty on the inside. I'm not afraid of her burning me. She couldn't; she's mine. Her dark brown eyes spill over with tears. Dark brown eyes like two large chocolate morsels. My sweet, sweet, sugary, chocolate-chip angel.

Just one … just one … just one … just one…

A gun fires off a little too close for comfort, and the bang yanks me out of my trance. "Please," she pleads again. "Help me."

I scoop her up under my shoulder and help steady her on her feet. "Come on," I say. "I know a hiding place," and I lead her back to the barn.

I shut the barn door behind us to try to block out the sounds of commotion from the massacre in the field. The Honda's engine drones on, and I kneel down and help prop Red-hair's back up against the barn wall. I hold her hands tightly and stare into her large chocolate-colored eyes. She looks around dreamily. "Why are we in the barn?" she asks softly.

"This is the hiding place," I say.

Her face screws up with confusion. "Here? Why here? This is where we keep—"

"It's okay. We'll be safe here. Al told me about it." I inch in closer and rub the back of her neck.

"Al?" she asks. "Al?"

"Yes," I coax.

She pauses for a few seconds and continues to look around in the barn. Her eyes stop when she realizes one of the cars is running, and the dreamy, faraway look in her eyes starts to come into focus. "Al don't know about any of the hiding places," she mumbles under her breath, her brain starting to put the pieces of the puzzle together. She looks down at her hands and at her shirt, then her eyes slowly shift upward in my direction—at my face, at my eyes, at my Altered scar. Her eyes go wide with knowing, and a wave of terror darkens her face. "Hey! Who are you, anyway?" she says frantically.

I quickly clamp one hand over her mouth and squeeze the flesh of her neck with the other. She struggles against my hold, but she's weakened from whatever battle she fought in the farmhouse. In an instant, I'm on top of her. My knees pin her arms down, and I press the rest of my weight against her bloodied shirt. I use both hands to squeeze her throat, but really, I could have only used one. With every gurgled gasp she makes, the elevator in my stomach gets higher and higher. I anticipate the *ding* in my head to let me know I've reached the top level.

I try. I try so hard to hold back. To make it last. It's been so long. Her breath is hot. She pants every time I loosen my grip and let her hungrily suck her air in and out. But I'm just teasing her. This is for me. Lightheaded. Ecstatic. And she doesn't stop fighting back. Kicks. Wriggles. Writhes. I don't want her to hold still because that's too easy. Every movement she makes is a chase for me. *A dance.* She twists one way; I force her to another. I enjoy the back and forth.

And I try to hold back—just one more second until I can't stand it any longer, and I bend over to graze my teeth against the side of her face. She yelps in pain. Not a full-blown scream, because my teeth aren't that sharp and I haven't made that big an indentation on her. I think her brain is trying to understand what's happening to her because this isn't your typical Infected attack. She's scared, and confused, and…

Delicious.

I bend forward and bite at her again. This time, I keep the apple of her cheek firmly in my teeth and clamp down as hard as I can. The flesh bursts open in my mouth, flooding my tongue with her sweet blood. Sugar. Pure. I press her head in place on the floor so she's unable to move her upper body, and I suck hard on her open wound. This gives a whole new meaning to the term "sucking face," and I giggle on the inside, thinking of Josh and his whacky sayings and antics.

It's not just Josh that makes me giggle, though. It's the rush. The fever. The wave after wave of hot satisfaction filling that empty elevator car in my stomach. I pull back and look her over when she goes limp underneath me. In all honesty, I feel like I've sucked her cheek dry! My sweet, sweet sugar princess passed out from pain or shock or both. Tiny bits of skin feel like sand in my teeth. I know I have to finish the job. I know I have to make sure she's *dead* dead.

Jarrod bursts through the barn door—a tattered, red-and-brown stained mess. He breathes heavily but smiles from ear to ear. He looks at Red-hair and back at me. "You done here?" he asks.

I shake my head.

"So, finish!"

I shake my head again. "I'm done. But I don't want to leave her like … she'll change soon if I don't." I remember the guard on Plum Island, Galloway. She turned so fast; it was pretty impressive. I remember Dr. Trager and what happened to him when I bit off his fingers. The change had started pretty quickly, too. And when Jarrod bit the men at the Safe Zone, bedlam was upon us in a matter of seconds. I need to finish Red-hair off soon.

He wipes his mouth with the back of his hand. "Well, I'm done, too. Totally done!" He jerks his head in the direction of the massacre. "There's plenty out there that'll take her," and he walks behind me and grabs Red-hair's feet. I stand up, grab her arms, and we toss her floppy body out the door. Into the fray. Food for the animals.

We leave the door open as we go back into the barn and hop into the car.

"We good," Jarrod says, putting the car in drive.

My head swims. I'm more than good. I'm sated and relieved and happy and disgusted and full all at the same time. I give him a "thumbs-up" sign and spit out a mouthful of coagulating blood onto the car floor.

"Lilly!" I say desperately, almost forgetting our pregnant human companion.

He lowers his eyes and shakes his head ruefully. "Gone."

Gone.

"Infected?" I ask.

"No. Gone."

I grit my teeth and look out the window.

Good job, Griffin. You've failed yet again. The one thing you are good at is letting yourself down, that's for sure.

Jarrod peels out of the barn, through the body-strewn field and onto the dirt road that leads back to the highway. A funnel of dust puffs up behind the Honda, and as we drive away, I realize there aren't any human screams left to be heard. Just the gentle moans of the Infected howling in the night.

IKE A DOG BEING PUNISHED, I COWER IN THE front seat with my knees propped up and my face buried in the space between my thighs and chest. *Bad boy! Bad boy!* I yell at myself in my mind. Every ounce of me hates what I did, and every ounce of me loves it. I'm so ashamed for the act, but my body is thankful for the nourishment. It's a disgusting and confusing dichotomy, and I just want to forget about it and hide. Now more than ever, it's absolutely vital that I go back to the Brandon Hospital, the old Re-Assimilation Center. I have to find some peace there, some help, some solace. If Dr. Oswald is there, I know she will take care of me. I pray to Santa Claus that she is. She will know what to do. If she's still alive, that is. It's not the ideal place to be, I know, but the time I was there, I was safe and somewhat comfortable, and I was *contained*. I need to go back to where I started. Back to the beginning. It needs to end there.

I know I'm not right, and not just for the unnatural urges or the hunger I have, or for the killing of Red-hair. I'm not well. Something is happening inside me that feels alien. Something in me is changing, evolving.

I can't put my finger on it, but the cravings, the bleeding ear, the irrational thoughts, the swoon over the mere sight of human blood ... it doesn't add up or seem *right*. I *feel* wrong, and I can't conjure up the words to describe it properly. When I was infected and then when I was Altered, I don't know; it just never felt like *this*. Like the way I feel right now.

Whatever Trager did to me...

"Oh, Griffin!" Jarrod says, breaking my train of thought. "You should have seen what I did to that guy!"

I grunt into my thighs and refuse to look up at him, but in my mind's eye, I know he's smiling and giddy. He's going to regale me with his murderous exploits, and I'll listen and groan every now and then. Maybe it's a good thing to listen to him. It'll at least get me out of my own head for a bit.

"I showed that sonuvabitch a few things about screwing with me! He almost tore my eardrum to shreds when he fired that gun next to my head. Well, I had to pay him back for that one, ya know. When I was finished with him, he didn't have any ears left. I made sure that one didn't turn, either. I killed him real good."

"Mmmm hmmm," I mumble.

"It had been a real long time since I felt that ... that ... *alive*," he muses.

His sister's voice comes back into my mind: *He couldn't wait to be infected again. Said he wanted to mess people up real bad and stuff.*

I lift up my head to look at him. "Oh, is that what you call it?"

He ignores my comment and continues, "Like when we first changed. The first time. It was like an awakening! Freedom. Margo never understood that. Had way too much of a kind heart. Too much of a gentle soul. Too much of a delicate disposition."

He said he wanted to OD on Black Death so he would be permanently infected again.

"I remember our first kill when we were first changed." He snickers. "We were at my friend Brent's engagement party. It was some swanky party at some fancy banquet place."

Yes, I know, you've told me the story before.

"Out of nowhere, this cold blast of air comes out of the A/C vents, and Margo says to me, 'Gee, that's weird that they would turn the air conditioning on in November.' Before I had the chance to answer her, the crash happened, followed by an explosion. So, we all rushed outside to see what happened. Not even thirty seconds of being out there, some asshole Infected bites her on the neck from behind. Margo was screaming and screaming, you know that sound, right? I turned around, ready to kill the guy with my bare hands. Of course, I had no clue what was really going on, ya know? Before I get a swing in, I get bum-rushed from the other side. Some chick tried to tackle me. I flung her to the side, but not before she chomped down on my hand." He holds up his hand to show me his original scar.

"Margo was bitten first, and in the neck, so she changed super-fast. It took me a little while to complete the change. I remember all that black goo pouring out of my mouth like water gushing out of a hose. So, I'm still going through it, and she's sniffing around me like a hungry animal, screeching, hooting, and hollering. She dips her friggin' hands into my black goo and starts smearing her face with it. She was out of her mind! I don't think her body knew what to do, ya know? She was like, confused and shit.

"And that hunger, that goddamn gnawing hunger, got me even before the full transformation. When I finally stood up, I kinda knew what was what. I just *knew*. And I showed her. There were still live humans inside the catering hall. I could smell them. My eyes hadn't fully changed but I knew what we had to do. I shoved Margo on top of one of the arrogant security guards. He was the guy who had given me static about the clip on my keyring. Said it was considered a weapon by the venue's standards. Stupid prick. Thought he was God or something making me go back to my car to lock up my goddamn keyring!"

Hated all people. Looked at them as cows. He was filled with so much rage and hate against everyone.

"So poor Margo was stunned when she fell on top of him. Poor, infected, clueless Margo! She had no idea! I did what any brother would do—I jumped in and helped her out. Started tearing at the guy's arm, biting into the bicep. She watched me for a minute or so and realized that's what she needed to do. I swear it was like teaching a little baby how to eat!" He laughs again and bangs his hand on the steering wheel with a yelp. "That's how I felt at the compound tonight! What about you?"

I rest my head on the tops of my knees. "I dunno," I lie. I want to push it out of my memory, want to bite down and squash it forever. Certainly not my proudest moment, considering I had been done with all that—ya know, eating people.

"No, I mean, what happened to you during your first time? How did it all go down on your end?" he presses.

I can't tell him. I don't have the heart. I don't have the desire to rehash it all. I don't want to tell him how my sister got tossed in the air like a ragdoll, and how my mother got mauled trying to save her. I don't want to tell him of my failed mission and how I was bitten on the neck from behind trying to sneak out and retrieve my car at the mechanic's place. I don't want to tell him about trashy Toby Youngblood and how I left a string of blood pearls around her neck but made sure she was *dead* dead.

"I don't really remember," I say quietly. "It was so long ago."

He sighs. "Well, I don't know about you, but I don't want this feeling to end."

Of course you don't, but I do. Looking back on my report card, I think it's safe to say I'm failing at this life thing. Not a single thing I've done has ever worked out or benefited anyone. I'm nothing but an animal. A monster.

The slow, harsh reality of my meaningless existence pricks at the base of my skull. When I was a human, I did nothing, accomplished nothing—except whine about my sister and having to ride a stupid school bus, and perfecting my daydreams of Lana Anderson. I wreaked havoc when I was Infected. Even when I tried so hard, I couldn't control myself, so I was a failure at that. And then as an Altered, I tried to keep Holston's memory alive by keeping his Altered children in check, and well, that landed me in an experimental cell. Now I can add Lilly and her unborn child to the list, even though they're probably better off dead. What good am I to anyone? I have to face it—I don't matter or mean a thing. I guess my one last hope is to go home to the center and live out the rest of my days alone.

"Still, though," I say, "don't you think the feelings we have aren't normal? Unnatural?"

"Face it, Griffin; we're *not* normal. Never gonna be normal. Now it's different because we can actually enjoy doing what we do best."

Killing.

"Enjoy it? What do you mean by that?"

"Think about it—we were wild when we were first infected. We were all crazy-like. In a fog. You remember. Some things from that time are so clear to me, and other things are just a blur, like I was on acid or something. We had a degree of awareness, but now? Griffin! We got it made! We're fully aware. We're fully in control. Why should we deny that part of us?"

"You mean the part that Trager engineered? It's not natural, Jarrod. You have to at least agree with me on that."

"Who's to say it isn't natural? Maybe it is. Maybe what Trager did to us just enhanced that side of us."

He was filled with so much rage and hate against everyone. I shake my head. "What Trager did to us is disgusting. What he did to all of us."

Dr. Trager. It all goes back to him. I know he is the one mainly responsible for everything that's happened. Sure, he had help from his cronies, most notably his main admirer, Dr. Rennard, and I would go so far as to say that Dr. Holston doesn't get off scot-free in the blame department, either. But Trager was the mastermind behind it all. He was responsible for the manipulation of the U Virus, and the release of the Zorna flu. He was responsible for the Plum Island experiments, and I wouldn't doubt if he was responsible for the manufacturing and distribution of the Black Death. He undermined all of

Holston's work and findings and set out to create a new world. Trager was determined to see this world burn for whatever reasons he had. Traumatic childhood? Daddy issues? Inferiority complex? God complex? Who knows. It doesn't matter now. Trager's running around infected on Plum Island with half a hand (thanks to me) and white eyes, mindlessly moaning and feasting on whatever life is left over there. Or he's dead. If Dr. Rennard had any sense left in her twisted brain, she would have put him down before he turned and then turned the gun on her shameful, Altered self.

The day flies by as we make our way from Virginia to Florida. It's a rather uneventful day as we stop periodically for gas and food. But who am I kidding? I'm not hungry, at least not like that. A bag of stale potato chips does little to sate my appetite when all I can think about is the warm rush of blood from Red-hair's cheek filling my mouth. Somewhere in Georgia, we come to a souvenir shop next to a gas station, and we both agree it's best to change out of our clothes. There's an old water-well around the back of the shop, and we rinse off with the icy water—washing away the strong scent of dried blood. The aroma no longer tugs at my senses, and I hope this will calm my growing hunger.

When we start seeing signs for Jacksonville, Florida, in the late afternoon, I immediately demand Jarrod let me drive. He pulls over and hesitantly lets me take the wheel. "You sure you're cool with this?" he asks.

"Of course. Not much longer now."

I'm home, in my home state, and I pretty much know the way from here. It's about a three-hour drive from Jacksonville to Tampa, and if I hustle enough, I can get the Honda there even sooner.

I roll down the windows to let the fresh air fill the car, to feel the warmth of a November night like you can only feel in Florida. Jarrod talks about hunting again, and I try so hard to tune him out. It's his hunger talking, I assume, and as he goes on and on, I feel my own hunger rising in the center of my chest like heartburn. It's a stabbing pang of hunger and guilt rolled into one. Cause I don't want to feel this way, don't want to feel…

"So, what's this place like?" he asks.

"The hospital?"

"Yeah, this Emerald City you've been jabbering on and on about since I met you."

I have to choose my words carefully. "It's secure. Decent fortification. Lots of supplies. I know they have a generator, so if there's any order there, they should have the basic necessities."

"Order? You remember the Safe Zone, right? Or do I have to remind you?"

I wave my hand in the air. "It's not like that. They have people and stuff who know things."

"Like from the first outbreak?"

I pause. Hesitate. Pick my words. He senses this. "Yeah."

"Like medicines and doctors?"

"Well, it is a hospital…" My voice trails off with a high-pitched tone.

"But they're equipped to handle this kind of stuff? And this is where your doctor friend is? And that kid?"

He's poking too hard, and I realize I have to tell him where we're going and what the implications of that are. I have to come clean about what happened to me because when we get there, I don't think I'll be able to keep my secret. All it will take is one person to recognize me, and the jig will be up. I was lucky enough to get this far without having to confess.

"Yeah. The doctor should be there. Dr. Oswald. And if all is well, she should have Troy with her, too."

He shifts in his seat. "So, refresh my memory, this Dr. Oswald—you said she was some kind of an Altered sympathizer, right?"

"Mmmm hmmm. She'll help us. She was willing to help me back then, and I don't see why that would change now."

"And you came to know her because she was running tests on that weird kid."

"Something like that."

"He was born at the Re-Assimilation Center? So how does that connect to you?"

"I used to run with a bunch of Altereds. Treatment and monitoring was offered to all Altereds in my area, not just those from the centers, so we just all kinda clicked together, I guess. Weren't there any Alt Homes near you?"

Jarrod bursts out with hearty laughter. "Alt Homes? Are you shitting me, Griffin? I don't know what kind of la-la fairy tale story you lived in Florida, but in New York, Alt Home was a joke! Bringing Altereds of all kinds together in a safe environment, that was the biggest farce out there. I went to an Alt Home out in Queens twice. Both times, I got jumped by humans who were protesting in the parking lot. That crazy old doctor who set that shit up ... what was his name again?"

"Holston."

"Yeah, yeah, Holston. He was a kook. He made a local commercial advertising the Alt Home. Real low budget.

Cheesy as hell. I only went cause I was hoping he would be there. Wanted to punch that asshole in the nose."

My blood screams, and I tighten my grip on the steering wheel. He definitely struck a nerve in me. If he only knew. If he only knew half of what Holston did for our kind, and even before we were Altered. Holston was a great man who sacrificed his life for the safety and well-being of humankind. He believed he was doing the right thing when he organized the Alt Homes. Hell, he funded them with most of his own money! He did what he could with what he had, and he only had the best intentions of the people in mind. To hear Jarrod speak ill of the doctor drives me to the brink of insanity.

My knuckles go white, and I can't hold it back anymore. "Look, Jarrod, the hospital we're going to is one of the original Re-Assimilation Centers."

Jarrod cocks his head to the side, and a croak escapes his throat.

"I know the place well because that's where they brought me." I pause. "The first time."

He leans forward, drums his fingers on the dashboard, and shakes his head wildly. "Wait wait wait! What are you saying? You were treated?"

"After the first outbreak. Yes. I was injected and was one of the first to wake up. They carted me off to the center where I was treated and rehabilitated and..."

He smashes his fists against the side of the door and rocks back and forth with disbelief. "So, you're a RAT? You're a goddamn Black Blood? Is that what you're telling me, Griffin?"

"Call it whatever you want," I respond calmly.

Suddenly, he reaches over and pulls on the wheel.

The car veers off the side of the interstate, and I slam hard on the brakes, causing us to spin into the opposite direction. Before I know it, Jarrod is out of the car and on my side in a flash. He reaches through the window, unlocks my door, and drags me out of the car.

And he punches me square in the face. I sway and stagger from the shock.

"All this time! All this time!"

He hits me again, and I fall onto my back. In a flash he's on top of me, knees pinning down my arms, his weight suffocating my chest. He wails on me relentlessly— punching my face, the side of my head, gripping his hands around my throat and violently shaking me. I try to fight back, but somehow this scene seems familiar. Not too long ago, I mounted a helpless woman and exerted my murderous will onto her, only this time I'm on the receiving end. The deserving receiving end. This is payback for my previous transgressions, and something like a smile forces its way onto my swollen face.

He's crying, trembling, screaming, "All this time! All this fucking time!" like I've wronged him in the vilest way possible.

One punch for Josh—my best friend who I abandoned as he was being torn to shreds.

One punch for Sydney—my sister who tried to stop me from getting my car and who ended up being tossed into the air like a ragdoll.

One punch for my mom—who screamed like a banshee as the Infected descended upon her, and I was powerless to help.

One punch for Toby—who crumbled under the weight of my infected hands as my first kill.

One punch for Holston—my pseudo-father who asked one simple thing of me that I could not fulfill.

Griffin, when I'm gone, I need you to be my eyes and ears. I need you to watch over them, protect them, for they are all my children. I'm going to need you to take care of the Altered.

One punch for Amber—the Altered girl who I thought could be my soulmate. I left her chained up and re-infected in a dilapidated drug house with strange people.

My vision goes blurry with each blow I take, but the faces of those I cared so much about haunt my distorted sight. Through the haziness and the furious roundhouse wailing of Jarrod's fists, I see his face come into view, mixed with the others of my memories, and it suddenly dawns on me ... I know why I keep him around—*I need to help him. I need to save him.*

I turn my head to the side and spit out a mouthful of blood. Blood mixed with black bile from the depths of my infected stomach—blood and black bile and bits of Red-hair's face that went undigested in my bowels. This snaps Jarrod back into the present, and he stops his assault and jumps off my chest. I roll over and spew up some more of the foul substance. Jarrod crouches on the balls of his feet and pants hard.

"I'm sorry. I'm sorry. I'm sorry," he repeats uncontrollably.

"It's okay," I mutter as I spit the last of it out. Because, really, it is. I deserved it. Needed it. My stomach isn't growling anymore. Jarrod literally beat the hunger out of me.

"I'm sorry, Griffin. I don't know what came over me, I..."

"Your ear," I say and point at him. "It's bleeding."

Startled, he reaches up and wipes his right ear. "Is this your blood?"

"I don't think so. Mine is all black and shitty."

His mouth drops, and the color in his cheeks goes stark white. "Griffin? What's happening to me?" he says like a child. Like a scared and helpless child.

Branches crack in the wooded area off the interstate, and our Altered senses hear it at the exact same time.

"Infected?" I suggest.

He gets up and stands over me. "We need to get out of here." He extends his hand to help me up.

13

COMING HOME AFTER A LONG DAY OF SCHOOL was always a treat. Depending on their schedules, sometimes my mother would be wrapping up her book club session, and the house would be filled with her laughter or words of wisdom. Sometimes, Sydney would be having a piano lesson, and music would drone on sweetly throughout the late afternoon. Sometimes, there would be freshly baked brownies just coming out of the oven for an afternoon snack. And sometimes, there was silence, and I would be the only one to enjoy the stillness of the large house. Whatever the scenario, we had a strict routine. It didn't matter what was going on, where we were, or who was over, but once the clock struck a certain hour, we all anxiously awaited the arrival of my father. When he got home from work, we ate dinner, had some family time, then did our own nightly rituals, but I'll never forget those moments of heightened anticipation right before he arrived. Did he have a good day or was he in a bad mood? Was he super stressed out or was he in good spirits? You never knew until he actually walked through the door and greeted us. My mother taught Sydney and me to recognize the timbre of his voice when he called from the garage door, "I'm home!" The tune in his words was a dead giveaway. And from that, Sydney and I adjusted our attitudes accordingly. Mom, too. And that's how I learned a valuable lesson—*it's not what you say, but how you say it*. The significance of that has become even greater since I became Altered.

When I walked out of the Re-Assimilation Center all those years ago, I never expected to be back under similar circumstances. I had gotten a job at the Brandon Medical Center, which is close to the hospital, but never had a need to go back to the hospital itself. The medical center was for checkups and bloodwork and specialist visits—nothing major. The hospital was for emergencies, surgeries, births, and anything else that fell under the emergency umbrella. When I was Altered, the hospital became my new home. I'd never gone back to my parents' home, and the Re-Assimilation Center was where my Altered self, my new self, was born and raised. Coming back to the center now felt strange.

I circle the car around the block a few times and tell Jarrod to pay close attention to what's happening in the windows. The hospital is five stories high, which makes us down below easy targets. For the most part, the windows are all shut tight and darkened out. I drive to the parking garage and leave the car on one of the mid-decks so we're not completely out in the open. It also gives us easy access so we can make a break for it in case we need to get out of there quickly.

We sneak around to the emergency room entranceway in the back part of the hospital grounds. With every footstep I take, I can't help but think we will be shot down at any given moment. As if reading my mind, Jarrod comments from the side of his mouth, "You know we're being watched, right?"

"Uh huh."

"Through scopes."

I shift my head in an upward direction. "I know. Third floor. I've never been shot before. What about you?"

"Nope. And I don't plan on it anytime soon."

I know we need to be deliberate and careful with our actions because I don't want whoever is watching to perceive us as Infected, or erratic humans. Walk too slowly, and they'll shoot us down. Walk too quickly, and they'll shoot us down. And we can't make too much noise because we don't want to attract any Infected in the area or alert any dangerous humans. We're in a no-win situation, and it's just a matter of time before...

"Who are you? What do you want?" a voice blares over a static-y bullhorn.

Jarrod and I both look to the sky to try and locate where it's coming from.

Third floor. I was right.

I put up my hands in a surrendering gesture. "We're looking for Dr. Dorothy Oswald," I say, my voice echoing off the side of the building. "She knows me from before all this."

"Who are you?" the semi-mechanical voice repeats.

"My name is Griffin King, 024. I'm a registered Altered and was once a patient here when the hospital was the Re-Assimilation Center. This is Jarrod Emerson, also an Altered. We're not hurt. We're not infected."

Jarrod nudges me with his elbow.

"Stop!" I admonish from the side of my mouth. "Is Dr. Oswald here?" Cause if she was still alive, she would have to be here.

No response.

"Do you know Dr. Oswald?"

No response.

I'm frustrated. Scared. I'm afraid they're going to shoot us or send us away. At this point, I'm not sure which would be worse. Name-dropping doesn't seem to be doing any good right now, but maybe I'm dropping the wrong name?

"Is a little boy named Troy here? I need to know if Troy McKenna is okay."

The person with the bullhorn releases the button ending the static feedback. After a few moments, it returns and says, "Hold on. Don't move. Stay exactly where you are."

Jarrod's eyes widen. "We're in? You think they're here?"

I try to smile, but the one side of my face where Jarrod hit me is too swollen to move. "I think so."

I hope so.

"If the doctor is here, what do you think she'll be able to do for us? How is she going to help us?" Jarrod asks.

"Holston was a smart man. He set this place up to be a Re-Assimilation Center, and I know in his grand design, he had every intention of keeping it that way. When it went back to 'hospital status,' I think the long-term emergency back-up plan was to use it as a center again if needed."

He shrugs. "What does that have to do with Oswald?"

"She knows his files. Knows how this place was intended to operate. They have labs and equipment and rooms set up so that people can have privacy. But most importantly, they're fortified and equipped to sustain the worst. We'll be safe here, at the least. I hope Oswald will be able to run tests on us to see what's going on—to tell us exactly what Trager did to us."

Jarrod fidgets in place. This revelation doesn't sit well with his killer instinct. He doesn't want to be caged or fortified or in some room to enjoy his privacy. He wants to run and hunt and howl against a moonlit sky. He wants to indulge in his predatory instincts and kill homeless men in Lettuce Lake Park and bathe in the blood of sewer cats because he can, and there isn't a person roaming the earth— Infected, Normal, or Altered—who can stop him.

Before he has a chance to express his discontent, four people in white hazmat suits come out of the ER door. Blue stitched letters read "CDC" on their lapels and their faces are covered in alien-esque face masks. Like the day in the city street. Like the day we were gassed and injected and hauled off. Like the day I was Altered...

"Hey! Hey! What are you doing?" Jarrod screams, as two of them surround and probe him. They push his head down to examine the back of his neck. They lift up his shirt and spin him around to check his stomach, chest, and back. They roll up his sleeves and stop there. I see as plain as day large teeth marks on his forearm. He must have been bitten during the attack on the Prepper camp in Virginia. Quickly, they fold his arms behind his back and clamp a set of handcuffs on his wrists. Jarrod bucks and screams and curses at them, calling them every name imaginable, spitting and kicking, flailing as much as he can.

Stop it! Stop it! Stop it! I scream at him from the inside.

"What the hell are they doing to me, Griffin? I'm not Infected! I'm fine! I'm fine! Don't you see my scar, you assholes! I'm Altered! I can't be re-infected."

Stop it! Stop it! Stop it! I say on the inside again.

He growls and snarls and chomps his teeth at them like an animal. "Griffin! Tell them! We can't be re-infected!"

They drag Jarrod inside the hospital while the other two white suits grab at me and give me the same treatment. They even tell me to drop my pants. When they see the two bites on my upper body, they place me in cuffs as well and walk me calmly inside.

I look around and observe the ER waiting room. There's a young woman wearing a lab coat behind the check-in desk. She clutches her shirt collar when she sees me and presses a button to close the doors behind us. My Altered senses pick up on the way the hospital feels— desolate, quiet. Hauntingly quiet—other than Jarrod's screaming and cursing, that is. A stagnant smell sits heavy in the air, as if the fresh November breeze hasn't blown through the corridors once. It smells and sounds like *sickness*. Not quite *infection*, but a sickness that I can't identify.

"Where are they taking my friend?" I ask.

They take off their face gear.

"To the observation room. To be sure," one of them replies.

They'll have much to observe, that's for sure. If the observation room is still the way I remember—with the cold floor, the stark white walls, the two-way mirror—I'm not sure how Jarrod is going to hold up. The memory of Trager's torture rooms might trigger him into insanity. He won't be the model test subject, even if the observations they make are for the greater good. If he gets too out of control, God only knows what they'll do to him.

They walk me to a conference room by the cafeteria on the first floor. The walls are a shade of baby blue, and there are off-white vertical blinds decorating the windows. I sit down in a metal folding chair at a six-foot table facing the entrance. Light shines in from the hallway through the long rectangular pane of glass in the door.

"Why did you bring me here?" I ask. "Where's Troy? Where's Dr. Oswald? Do you know Dr. Oswald?"

"She runs this place," one of them responds. "Dr. Oz has been in charge since the beginning of the second outbreak."

My muscles relax, and a calm wave washes over me. I think I smile, but my face is throbbing so badly that I don't quite know what expression it makes.

She's here. I made it.

"And the boy? Troy?"

The two of them glance at each other, telling each other with the mere look of their eyes to not say a word about him. My senses twitch at their suspicious exchange. "The doctor is busy with a patient right now. She'll be with you in a little bit." They look at each other again, remove my cuffs, and leave.

I sit back in the chair, close my eyes, and exhale. A sigh of relief. A sigh of accomplishment. I made it. I did it. Troy is here, and Oswald is here, and I'll be able to tell her what happened to us and get some answers. She'll be able to help me. She'll be able to help me control my growing hunger and rage. I'm home. I made it.

Behind my closed eyes, I sense the light from the pane of the door-glass darkening, and I sit up at attention but don't open my eyes. I wait it out. It opens slowly, and the tall shadow hovers in the doorway for a minute, like a looming cloud of darkness threatening a clear blue sky. I smell the cologne before the figure even steps over the threshold, and I open my eyes when the deep, bassy voice announces, "Well, well, well. Holston's prodigal son returns."

My heart stops at the sound of his voice, like ghostly hands wringing around every muscle in my chest. It feels heavy and hard to breathe. That voice. A voice that is forever ingrained upon my memory. Gooseflesh ripples down my arms like slime oozing down my body. Every hair on the nape of my neck stands at attention. That voice. A voice that can calm a tidal wave in its very tracks or can enchant Altereds to suicide (or so the legend goes). The deep bass notes belong to only one man...

Graves.

He saunters into the room, closing the door behind him, and sits at the conference table across from me. I stare him down, drinking in his features, sizing up his movements. I watch him both defensively and offensively—ready to strike if he provokes me, ready to defend if he threatens me. His artificial fragrance masks his natural scent, and I can't decide what foods he actually smells like. As usual, his black hair is slicked back with gel. He's gotten even grayer around his temples since the last time I saw him, and his skin still has the bronze glow of an unnatural tan. The cologne, hair product, and UV-embedded flesh is overpowering. They dull my hunger with a nauseated feeling. I chuckle because I finally realize these are his defense mechanisms. Perhaps the only way he's survived both outbreaks—no Infected wants to eat through a mouthful of chemicals!

His presence takes me off guard as his sinister black eyes burn holes right through me. Not in a million years did I think I would ever see him again, and now that he's in front of me, I don't know what to say to him. The last time I had seen him, I was spilling my guts out about Black Death and Eugene and the Ferals. He assured me I would be safe. Well, we all know how that turned out. Soon after I had met with him, I was drugged up and on a plane to Plum Island!

"What are you doing here?" I growl.

He licks his lips, and every muscle pulls tightly against his face. Nothing about him has changed—he's the same Lord Hades, Warren J. Graves as he's always been, except this time there's no clipboard or tape recorder attached to him.

"I was going to ask the same of you, 24." He's goading me—purposefully calling me my Altered identity name to get a rise out of me. If I had a dollar for every time I wanted to reach across a table—any table— and tear his face off, I'd be a rich man! "Where have you been, buddy?" he sneers.

I refuse to fall into his trap. "Where's Dr. Oswald?" I say dryly.

"Making her rounds. She'll be by in a little bit. She was worried about you."

"Yeah? Did you explain to her how you ratted me out?"

He pulls back a little, as if I've verbally struck him in his chiseled face. "What are you talking about?"

I cross my arms in front of my chest. "You gave me up to Trager; don't deny it."

He shakes his head. "No. I didn't."

"Bullshit!" I bark as my body lurches forward. "I opened up to you, and you promised nothing would happen to me and..."

"And you went missing," he interrupts, his voice rising slightly above mine. I cower uncontrollably at the sound of it and sink back into the chair. "You disappeared. Dr. Oswald..." he pauses, hesitates, swallows hard in his throat, "... and I," he emphasizes slowly, "searched for you."

My eyebrows rise in disbelief. *He* looked for *me*? Yeah. Right. If that's true, then I'm a human! There's no way Graves would spend any of his precious time worrying about me! I stifle a maniacal laughing fit. "Why don't I believe you? You knew exactly where I was."

His black eyes go darker as he drums his fingers on the table. "It didn't take long to figure out where you might have been, but then everything unfolded quickly, and by the time we were able to organize, the second outbreak exploded. I chose to stay with Dr. Oswald at the hospital to manage things. What happened to you? How did you get back here?"

There's a genuine solemnity in his voice, but my walls are so high and so thick with concrete. "I ain't telling you shit."

He chuckles deep in his chest and bops his head up and down. "I figured you would say that."

"Why are you helping Oswald, anyway? I thought you were the 'victim-whisperer' or something?"

"Or something." He exhales. "You know Dr. Holston and I were not just colleagues, but close friends. He and I believed in the same cause..."

"If I remember correctly, you shut him down."

"Friends are allowed to disagree," he defends. "I still think Peter's work was of the utmost importance, and if I can help his legacy, help his work by assisting Oswald, then it's my duty and obligation to do it."

"What legacy?" I sneer. "The preservation of mankind?"

Something flashes in his side smirk and my Altered senses tingle. In the past, I think I'd been a pretty good judge of Graves's intentions, but now I'm not so sure. He's thrown me for one hell of a loop and once again, I'm the bug, and he's the size fifteen shoe taunting me, waiting to get me in the trap, waiting to crush me under the thick sole.

He narrows his eyes, rests his elbows on the table, and brings his clasped hands in front of his mouth. "Or something," he says ominously.

HERE HE IS! THE GRAVES I'VE GROWN TO know and hate and love and respect and want to kill and admire and loathe. There's that glimmer, that shine of deep-seated hatred underneath his carefully manicured veneer. He finally sits back in the chair and crosses his arms over his chest as if he and I are in some bizarre version of a Mexican standoff. "You're really not going to talk to me?" he asks with mock concern.

"Nope. Psycho-babble 101 is not gonna work this time. I told you, I ain't telling you a thing." Because even though he's denied it, a part of me still believes he sold me out to Trager.

His slithery snake smile curves up at the corners of his mouth. "C'mon, 24, you've always been the talkative type."

I huff. He's still trying to rile me up, hoping that I'll spew out all my information if I'm in a pissed-off mood. But I know him too well and learned enough about myself in the process to not fall victim to his Jedi mind tricks anymore. There's a reason why he's good at what he does, but I'm on to him. He can't manipulate me anymore. "Nice try, Graves. Things are different now. I'm different now."

"We shall see." He relaxes his shoulders.

We sit in silence for what feels like an hour. Staring at each other. Neither of us budging or making an attempt to engage the other in conversation. My palms get sweaty from the tension, but I wipe them down the fronts of my jeans. Every now and then, Graves shifts his legs, or rests his elbows on the table, or tilts his head from side to side to show off the loud, strong bones cracking in his neck. But neither of us says a word.

Soon, there's a knock on the door, and Graves swivels his head to see who it is. He nods, and the door opens. An orderly pops his head in and says, "Oswald says to bring him to her. She got caught up and is running behind."

Graves dismisses the orderly and stands up. The massive build of his body rises like a stone monolith from the earth. His black shirt and black silk tie serve as a nice contrast against his neatly pressed gray suit jacket and slacks. I wonder how he's able to stay so well-put-together amidst the end of the world.

With his fore and middle fingers, he motions "come here" at me, and I begrudgingly get up at his command. He leads me out of the conference room and down the hallway until we reach the elevator lift and stairwell. He opens the door to the stairs and starts to go in, but I freeze. Why isn't he taking us on the elevator? I know they're running off the solar power and generator, so why are we hoofin' it?

He senses my hesitation and sighs. "I'm not going to hurt you, or push you down the stairs, or beat you up, or anything like that, if that's what you're thinking. Besides, it looks like you've had plenty of that on your own."

My hand shoots up to touch the side of my puffed-up face.

"We don't use the elevators because it's not safe to. If one broke down, or someone got stuck, it would be more trouble than it's worth. The elevators are for emergencies only or for heavy transport that can't get up or down by stairs."

I nod tersely and follow him up the steps to the second floor. Oswald's office is next to the stairwell, so Graves opens the door and half-shoves me inside. "See you soon, 24," he sings, and he turns on his heels and walks back down the staircase.

Oswald paces back and forth in front of her desk, and she doesn't even realize the door opened and that I'm standing there. Her sandy blonde hair is pulled back into a ponytail, and the only word I can use to describe the expression on her face is *worried*. There's a certain anxious sway in her hips, a nervousness as she nibbles furiously at the sides of her fingers. Each one goes in her mouth, and she gnaws at the skin with mouse-like motions. My stomach rumbles, but it's a low growl that only I hear. She smells like cake, and each morsel of flesh she rips from her fingertips smells like sugary frosting. I swallow hard to suppress the thoughts.

"Knock knock," I say.

She stops in her tracks and looks up from her hand. Her eyes light up with pure happiness when she sees me, and she exhales a sigh of relief. "Oh my word!" she gushes. "Griffin! Where have you been?" In a swift motion, she glides across the floor with her arms outstretched and pulls me into her embrace. "Oh my God! Oh my God! I was so worried about you. So worried!" she says over and over into my shoulder.

Oswald locks her arms within mine, and I pull my head back just enough to meet her gaze. "Troy? Crystal?"

She nods. "They're here. They're safe. Oh lord!" She gasps. "Look at you! You're hurt! What happened?"

I chuckle. "I'm fine. You should see the other guy."

She laughs and breaks her hold on me. "Please, sit down. Tell me everything. Where were you? How did you get back home?"

I sit on the couch across from her desk, and she sits at the opposite end. "No. What happened here? Please. I need to know."

She crosses her legs and slumps forward onto her lap. "Oh, Griffin," she moans, exasperated. "Where do I begin?"

"Troy. Crystal."

She sits up and breathes deeply. "Okay. It was a few days after I met with you and Troy and Crystal in your apartment. Crystal called me in the middle of the night saying that she was afraid for their lives. I had just assumed she was talking about the three of you. I thought you may have been hurt because she was the one calling me. I immediately rushed over to see how I could help out, and that's when she told me you had been abducted."

"Dr. Trager. Well, not him specifically, but his people—two security guards and another doctor. Dr. Rennard. She was Altered, too."

She rubs her face in her hands, but the second I say Rennard's name, an icy stare glazes her eyes. "An Altered woman? Rennard? Short blonde hair? About my age? Very cold?"

"Yeah. Why?"

She sits back against the cushion. There's a far-away look in her eyes. "Hmmm..." Her voice trails off in thought.

"So what happened next?" I say, breaking her concentration.

She snaps her head back to me. "Oh, I ... uh ... I took Troy and Crystal back to my house that night and called Warren."

"*Graves*? You trusted him?"

"Yes," she replies, shocked. "Why wouldn't I trust him? He was one of my uncle's closest friends. If *he* trusted him, I had to, as well."

"But he's the one who gave me up to Trager!" I roar. "You can't trust Graves! I went through hell because of him!"

"No, Griffin, you're wrong. Warren didn't do anything like that."

"He had to have. He's hated me from the beginning. Me and the famous Doctor Warren J. Graves go back a *long* time, and trust me, we're not bosom buddies, if you know what I mean."

"No. No, he didn't. I..." Something in her tone shifts, and she falters with her words. Stammers. Shakes. I smell salty sweat spring up on top of her eyebrows. "I..." she tries again. Hesitates. Thinks. Mulls. Squints her eyes. "I ... I think it was me."

"You what?" I roar in disbelief.

"The Altered doctor—Doctor Rennard. I met her at the Brandon Medical Center the day after my visit with you and Crystal and the baby. I was there to run labs on Troy's hair sample, and I don't even remember the circumstances, but she approached me praising my uncle and all the things he did for her as an Altered. She said she was going to be starting a job at the center and that she was sorry for my loss. I didn't think it strange at the time, but..."

"They followed you. Watched you. They were watching you the entire time." The picture comes into sight now. It's all clear, and I can't dwell on it. What happened, happened. He actually wasn't lying to me when he said he had nothing to do with it. I probably owe Graves an apology, but I know I'll never actually do it. The apology in my head will have to suffice because I don't ever want to show him weakness, or kindness, or sympathy again. Is Graves going soft? Have his thoughts and feelings toward me changed somehow?

I could only be so lucky.

She gasps, stifling down her tears. "Oh, Griffin! I'm so sorry!"

I wave my hand in the air. "What happened next? What happened when you called Graves?"

She stiffens up her back and smooths her hands down the front of her white lab coat. "Well," she says, composing herself, "Warren came by the next day, and we went over all my uncle's case files to try to figure out the logistics. We decided not to get the police involved because Crystal said it was Tampa PD who took you away, and we wanted to be as discreet as possible because of the larger implications. I took Crystal back to the house where she was staying with Eugene, and I had him organize a team of people to be on the lookout or keep their ears to the ground. I searched Altered message boards, Black Death reports, all of those types of things online. But nothing came up. And then Warren and I both agreed that the most obvious place had been staring us down the whole time."

"Plum Island," I interject.

She nods. "But by then, it was too late. Patients started coming in. Reports of Infected. *Children* with infection. The hospital didn't have enough isolation rooms to contain the sick people, and things got so out of control that it was difficult to tell whether someone was *infected* infected, or high, or OD'ing on Black Death. It wasn't just us, either. This was happening all over the country. All over the world."

"We heard a radio broadcast mention something about Denmark."

She nods and continues, "Warren had suggested that I contact some of Uncle Peter's old colleagues who worked with him on the U Virus and his manifesto. So, I did, and I told them that it felt like the pattern was starting all over again. The signs of a second outbreak happening, and happening fast, were all there. With the research and reports, we were able to present our case to the CDC and quickly got a federal injunction to take the hospital over as an emergency site, as per my uncle's guidelines and recommendations. And here we are."

"Emergency site? You mean like a Safe Zone?"

A pained expression comes over her. "No. Not at all. Most of the Safe Zones have fallen. They had good intentions, but they weren't ready or equipped for proper implementation."

"A Re-Assimilation Center?" I ask, but as soon as it comes out of my mouth, I hear Matt's voice in my head say, *"Why would they set up those? There isn't anyone to re- assimilate."*

Oswald shakes her head. "We're a research facility."

I shudder. The memory of Trager's experiments flood into my mind all at once. A whirlwind tornado of images and sounds and smells and sensations envelope me, and a rush of anger and confusion forces me to grip the side of the couch. What he took from me, what he did to me, I'd bite off hundreds of thousands of fingers to make that go away. I could start with Oswald. She does have ten sugary sweet ones for the taking.

"Research facility? That's what you're calling it? You're doing experiments on people, aren't you? Like Trager!" I dig in to the couch harder.

She recoils slightly on the opposite end. "No! Not at all." The tone of her voice switches to a gentler, calmer one. A trick she undoubtedly snagged from Graves. "There's a difference between experimenting and researching. No one knew what Trager was up to on that island. It was top-secret. Need-to-know-basis type of stuff. Not even my uncle knew."

"That's nice. Nice to know that you didn't get your doctor's degree from The Trager Institute of Plum Island." I try not to be sarcastic and mean to her, but I can't help it. I don't want to get into semantics. Research. Experiments. It's all the same, really. Every piece of paper I ever read from Holston's files was research, but you can't conduct that research without a level of experimentation. Word play; I hate it. I just want to be real right now. "What about my friend, Jarrod? Where did they take him?"

"He's in an observation room. The nurses looked him over, and he has some pretty bad scrapes and cuts. He also has some deep puncture wounds that are worrying. If they're bite marks from Infected, he would have shown signs but..." She trails off from her sentence. "They took his blood, and I'll be running some preliminary tests to be safe. I'll need to run some tests on you, too."

Yes, Dr. Oswald, they are bites from Infected. But Jarrod can't be re-infected. Neither can I.

"Hmmm," I mumble. "Well, you're gonna want to run a whole lot of tests on us."

"Why's that?"

"Plum Island. What Trager did to us."

"What do you mean?"

"He tested on us. Experimented on us the whole time. Said it was all in the name of research."

She shudders.

"And every day was a new test. I was forced to watch tortures, was tortured myself, given drugs to make me turn. Then, they chained me to a chair and flashed images in a viewfinder while they injected me with something. Daily. Jarrod, too."

"Injected you with what? Did they say? How did it make you feel?"

"I don't know. Zorna flu? Zombaxin? Zombaxin Plus, maybe? I have no clue. It made me feel … infected, I guess."

Pink worry flushes her face. "Okay, Griffin. I'll get you set up in an observation room right away. I'm so, so sorry." She stands up and reaches out for my hand.

"I want to see Troy," I say and stand up next to her.

"You can't."

My blood screams inside me. "Why? Why not!"

"He's in isolation."

"What do you mean *isolation*? He's not infected! He's just a little boy! Why would you do that?"

She puts her hand on my shoulder to calm me down. "I can't risk him, Griffin. You and I both know he's very important. The Infected went crazy just when they were in the room next to him. We eventually had to separate everyone by floor."

"You have Infected in the building?" I roar.

"Of course, Griffin. Infected, Altered, human."

"For research, right." I jerk my shoulder away from her touch. "Yeah, I hear ya. And you've locked a little boy up in isolation like he's some freak-o science fair experiment."

"He's the key, Griffin," she says, trying to coax me. "The key to a cure. A real cure. The eradication of the virus and all components of it. All the data points to it. I'm working day and night to come up with something, and quite honestly, I'm running out of options … and time."

Data shmata. Thoughts of Troy being experimented on drive me mad. I promised him I would protect him. I promised he would be okay. And now, he's here? Being analyzed and tested on like an animal. Alone and afraid. Away from his mother. Not able to understand what's going on around him. This is no life. No way for him to live and be raised. He should have a chance to be normal. A normal, little boy, playing little kid games and singing songs and eating cookies and milk for breakfast and watching TV, even when your father said it was too much, and growing up and worrying about going to prom with your life-long crush, Lana Anderson, and … I've come all this way, endured so much, and the pit of my stomach is on fire with hunger and rage, hunger and rage, hunger and rage. Maybe Troy isn't the key after all? Maybe he does have a shot at a semi-normal existence? Maybe Jarrod and I are the Frankenstein's monsters? Now that I'm home, maybe I'll be able to do some good? For once in my life.

I could only be so lucky.

"Test my blood, Doctor. Let's go, let's do it now."

She cocks her head to the side, confused.

"You might just find something interesting."

"What makes you say that?"

"Do I look infected to you, Dr. Oswald?"

She raises her eyebrows and gives me an "are-you-kidding-me" stare. "You're Altered, Griffin. There's no way you're infected."

"What if I told you I could bite you right now and you would turn?"

A humming noise rises from her throat and vibrates against her lips. "No. That's not possible. Besides, you don't have any outward signs of being infected."

I smirk. "Test me. You'll see."

SWALD SAID WE'RE NOT PRISONERS HERE. We're not even considered patients. She called us her guests. We have the freedom to come and go, but like anything, there are restricted areas of the hospital. Fine, I get that much. She also said we could leave whenever we wanted. Yeah? And go where? Unless she's completely oblivious to humankind's Extinction Event that is currently happening outside the hospital doors, then there really must be no hope for any of us.

Somehow I don't believe Oswald is that ignorant, nor does she take me for a fool. She's smart (I mean she was a pediatric surgeon for Christ's sake!), but she's also genuinely kind. She has an endearing bedside manner that is beyond compare. Like her patients see her coming into the room with her steel cart and trays of medicines and needles, and all other nasty medical crap, and they're practically taking off their clothes and throwing their arms in her face. "Please, Dr. Oz! You can stick me with that hot shot of antidote right now! Here, Dr. Oz! Tap this vein! It's been waiting for you all day!" When she escorted me to the lab to run my tests, it took forever to get to the room because everyone in the halls stopped to greet her or talk to her. She patted people on their backs and checked in with some of her favorite patients—some of the other Altereds staying in our wing. It's sweet trickery, I suppose. I call it *The Holston Effect*.

Now, *The Holston Effect* is not to be confused with *The Graves Effect*. *The Graves Effect* is much different, you see. Graves can manipulate you and work his way inside your brain and implant his own projections of the world. It's so subtle, too, almost like a subliminal message because the victim truly has no idea it's even happening. Then, out of his own spiteful accord, he'll drop a hint letting you know you've been tricked. So, you've not only been duped, but you have the knowledge of the manipulation, and you feel like a complete failure at life for allowing it to happen. *The Graves Effect—manipulation at its finest!* At least with Dr. Oswald and *The Holston Effect*, she could be lying to you, and you would never know it. A family trait. Her sympathetic eyes and gentle touch of her hand are the perfect combination for her brand of deception. It almost makes it okay in a super weird kind of way. Thinking about it now, I'm not sure which one is better, or which one is worse.

Regardless, what separates Oswald and Graves is basically the same thing that separated Holston and Graves. Oswald has compassion for the Altered, while Graves has nothing but contempt. The curious new development, or rather I should say the wrench in my "I-got-Graves- figured-out-decree" is the fact that he wasn't the one who turned me in to Trager. It was Oswald's inadvertent mistake. So, has his hatred for my kind subsided? Has the Grinch's heart grown three sizes? I guess I'll have to do more analysis the next time I'm around him, but I have a sneaking suspicion the next time I see him, he'll be doing some analysis of his own in his own Graves-y kind of way.

Oswald had brought me to a place she called the observation room, which was just a really nice way of saying lab. They ran me through a battery of tests—MRIs, X-rays, bloodwork, general physical, eye exam, hearing test—you name it, they did it. The nurses remarked that they haven't fired up the MRI machine since they took full shelter in the hospital, but apparently Oswald thought it was important enough to get it up and running for Jarrod and me, taking a nice, hard look at whatever is brewing in our insides.

After the testing, I was taken to my room in the Altered Wing. It's a regular patient room with white boards on the walls, two beds with a curtain between them, a desk, and a private bathroom. It's familiar. Not the room I stayed in when it was called the Re-Assimilation Center but similar. This is more like a short-term patient room for people who had minor surgery or an injury or needed to be monitored for a few days. This is an in-and-out kind of room. I can tell because there isn't any cutesy fake family pictures displayed or eclectic artwork hanging on the walls, ya know stuff that would make the room feel "homey" for anyone who would need to be here for an extended amount of time.

A loud commotion echoes from down the hallway, startling me out of my daydream. My muscles tighten up and I clench my fists, readying myself for something to come. As the voices get closer, I realize it's Jarrod— yelling, screaming, cursing, and being his usual wild self. When we were first on the road together, he was reserved and restrained for the most part. The closer we got to Florida, the more he seemed to spiral out of control. I can't help but wonder if Jarrod is going through a PTSD of sorts. I definitely know he can't stand doctors and tests and needles, and I know they did to him what they did to me. He's definitely not a happy camper.

The door flings open. "Screw you!" he yells at the guards as they shove him into the room. "You can't keep me here! You think you're gonna stick me with more of your needles? I'm so outta here!" He flails his body and spits on the floor, and for the first time in a long while, I hear his thick New York accent come out, like how my mother's did when she was enraged.

"If you want to go, you're free to go," one guard says nonchalantly while the other one snickers. "Dr. Oswald says you don't have to stay here, pal."

Jarrod crouches the upper half of his body like he's going to charge at them. He holds that position for a few seconds, then rises up and slams the door. "Stupid mother..." His voice trails off when he notices me sitting on one of the beds. "They get you, too?" He holds out his arms, revealing dark bruises in the centers of them.

"Not like that! They must have had trouble finding your vein."

"Yeah, they'll find a vein alright!" he barks at the door. I have no idea what he means by that. He sits on the edge of my bed and puts his head in his hands, rubbing his temples. "Man, what are we doing here? What the hell is going on? I know you wanted to see that doctor and the kid, but did you know they were going to do all that stuff to us?"

I shake my head. A sort of lie.

"This is Plum Island Light!" he barks.

"Oh stop!" I snap. "It wasn't that bad! Oswald needs us for her research."

He looks up from his hands. "So did Trager."

"This is different, Jarrod. We're safe here. She's not going to experiment on us or anything like that."

"Oh, no? Then why did she divide all the people up into 'wings'? The Infected Wing, the Altered Wing ... this whole operation is shady." He gets up from the bed, goes over to the door, and looks out the window up and down the hall.

"I don't know. Maybe it helps with her research? Maybe it's to keep people safe?"

He turns around and looks at me. His eyes blaze hot with anger, and he furrows his brows. "This is bullshit! You led us from one torture chamber to the next! I promise you I'm gonna get out of here!"

"Oh stop! You ain't going nowhere! We're not prisoners, but there's nothing for us out there. All we have is the now and here."

Something stirs inside me. I know when Jarrod starts talking about his anger, starts giving *in* to his anger, his hunger isn't too far behind. What we've become, what Trager made us, it's the most dangerous weapon there is right now, and if Jarrod loses control, if he loses himself to the hunger and gives in to it, it won't be long before this research facility falls just like every Safe Zone in this country. I have to keep an extra close eye on him so he doesn't run wild and start eating—and *changing*—people.

Even though Oswald is an Altered sympathizer, I didn't tell her about our feeding frenzy and constant hunger. I was afraid that if she knew, she would throw us in isolation so fast it would make our heads spin. She would say it was for our own safety or however she would sugarcoat it, but she would be scared, nonetheless. And her vision of us would change. Her vision of me would change. Now, if all the tests she did on us will paint that picture for her, then fine. But that was information I wasn't willing to voluntarily offer up.

"Nah, Griffin. I'm gonna leave. I can't stay locked up again." He turns back around and faces the door again. I know it's locked. They always lock it. I know what's going to happen, too. He's going to jiggle the handle, see that it's locked, and start pounding and wailing on the door, screaming like a mad man for someone to let him out and...

The door handle clicks open when he turns it, and my head shifts with curiosity. "It's not locked?" I whisper to myself, but his Altered senses hear me clear as day. I jump up from the bed and make my way next to him in the doorway, amazed that they actually didn't trap us in this room, in shock that Dr. Oswald actually meant that we...

"Not prisoners, my ass," Jarrod bellows when one of the guards at the nurses' station comes jogging over to our room.

He stands defensively in front of us in true military fashion—rifle clutched at the ready, legs spread apart. My brain registers his stance and understands that he's not letting us out of this room. "What can I do for you guys?" he asks in a monotone voice.

Jarrod and I glance at each other.

"I want to see a patient. Troy McKenna," I say firmly.

"He can't have any visitors. He's having his treatment."

"What about the day room on the fifth floor? We can go up there, right?"

The guard hesitates for a second, as if he's reading a schedule on a piece of paper in his mind. "Sure," he says and steps aside so we can slither out of the room.

He walks us up to the fifth floor and leaves us in the day room with a grunt. "Go straight back to your room when you're done," he says before walking back down the stairs.

As we had gone up every landing in the staircase though, I noticed something I hadn't before—this hospital is heavily armed. Secured. I've counted three armed guards in the stairwell alone. The atmosphere is very different from the first time around, too. Armed and guarded to the teeth on the inside so the big bads on the outside can't harm us, but oblivious to the dangers and big bads who dwell on the inside, looking to break free to the outside.

A scary thought enters my mind: *There is no safe place.* I shake my head like a dog with fleas, hoping to shake that notion away for good.

The day room hasn't changed much from the last time I was here. The same tables with the same board games and cards. The same desk in the center of the room and the same chairs set up in a circle for *group*. There are a few other people sitting on the couches and reading books. They're *people* people. Humans. No scars. It was awfully nice of Oswald to allow the two species to mingle together, albeit under constant armed surveillance. I'd be willing to bet she had to twist Graves's arm to let that fly.

"This is the day room," I say to Jarrod. "Not too exciting, but it's at least a place to hang out. They used to let us go outside to shoot hoops and get fresh air, but I don't think they'll let that happen now. Ya know? Second apocalypse and all."

Jarrod huffs out a little chuckle. I have to admit, I can be a funny guy sometimes.

"Lighting strike me dead right here and now!" a voice booms across the room.

Startled, I turn my head, and my entire body follows in succession. Before me is a sight I thought impossible to behold. My mouth drops as the two figures approach. I guess what they say is true—only cockroaches will survive the apocalypse.

"Eugene?" I yell out in disbelief. "Crystal?" My heart leaps in my chest, and I crane my neck to see if there's anyone with them—anyone else I left behind, anyone else like Amber...

Crystal's eyes light up when I meet her unexpected gaze, while Eugene claps me heartily on my back. "Dude! What the hell, man? What happened to you? We thought for sure you were dead!"

"Well, you can't get rid of me that easily," I joke, and Crystal's smile all but overcomes her entire face. She throws her skinny arms around my neck and squeezes me tightly.

Eugene's hand trembles as he swipes a strand of his long, greasy hair from his eyes. *I guess some things will never change, no matter what is happening in the world.* "Dude! You have no idea, man! No friggin' idea!"

"Oh, I think I have some clue," I say as Crystal unlocks her arms from me and goes back to attaching herself to Eugene like a magnet.

"No really. This time was different, man. This time was fast!" He gesticulates wildly, and I smile at him in spite of myself.

"Where did they take you?" Crystal squeaks in her high-pitched voice.

"A bad place. But you did good. You called Dr. Oswald and got Troy to safety."

She smiles so large again that I think she's going to split her face open.

"Eugene, Crystal, this is Jarrod," I introduce.

Eugene nods and points to Jarrod's Altered scar to acknowledge their kinship. Jarrod barely mutters out a "Hey."

Eugene tugs on my shirt sleeve. "So, c'mon, man! Tell me what went down!"

I sigh. "It's a long story. We were taken to an island, to a research facility."

Crystal tightens her grip on Eugene's arm and her face goes white when I say "research facility."

"No, no, no," I assure her. "Not like this one. A really bad one. They tortured me and Jarrod, but we were able to escape."

Eugene throws one hand around in the air. His putrid stench wafts in my nostrils, and even Jarrod takes a step back to avoid the smell. "And you came home to this!"

"Not funny, but yeah. I guess you're right. So, what happened on your end?"

Crystal makes a small chirping sound in her throat, and Eugene hangs his head low. "We lost everyone, man. Everyone's gone."

"Amber?" I manage to say.

"Most of the crew got killed. Jimmy's dead. Infected tore him up and left nothing to come back. Marco and your girl were in that room, ya know, riding out their high on Black Death. Well, we suspect that Marco got better, like he must have come down and wasn't infected no more. But there wasn't anyone around at the time to help him out. No one around to unlock that damn door. So, Amber ... well, she did a number on him, man. Tore him up to ribbons."

"Wait! The Infected don't eat the Altered!" I exclaim.

"Well, she sure did! I guess when you're hungry enough, you'll eat just about anything. Even sour meat. When we came home that day and found them, I had no other choice but to let her go."

"She was still infected? The Black Death was still in her?"

"Yep. She was never coming out of that, man. Never."

"And you just let her go? Let her run loose?"

Eugene's left eye twitches. "I mean, I wasn't gonna put down one of my own, ya know?"

So, Amber is still out there. Infected and running free.

A low grumbling noise erupts from someone's stomach, and we all turn to each other to see who it's coming from. The look on Jarrod's face gives it away, and Eugene laughs.

Jarrod is not amused, however. "How do you all know each other?" he sneers suspiciously.

"I told you about Eugene and the others," I say quickly before Eugene can get a word in.

But my plan backfires because Eugene gets a rush of nostalgia as he announces, "We were in this center together! 7," he points to Crystal, "16," he points to himself, "and good ole 24!" He points to me. "It was a crazy time, man! Super freakin' crazy!"

"You were in the Re-Assimilation Center, too?" Jarrod bellows with disbelief and disgust that I know exactly what his brain is thinking. He's thinking, *Why him and not me? Why this scumbag and mute and not me and Margo?* Jarrod's upper lip curls, and I know I'm going to have to intervene soon.

Eugene takes a step closer to me and leans in to my ear. *My bloody ear.* He takes his finger and smears the blood on the outside of my earlobe like he's finger-painting. I swat his hand away, "Stop! If you gotta tell me something, just say it."

"They're gonna nuke this place, ya know."

I pull back and Crystal squeaks again. "Shut up! You don't know what you're talking about."

His face twitches, and the bump of his scar swallows his eye. "Just sayin'. That's the word on the street."

"There's no way, Eugene! I saw a newspaper. They cancelled the election. The government is gone. There's nobody to press the red button."

"Shhhh!" he admonishes as his body convulses. "Keep your voice down! If they know we know..."

"You need to stop telling those stories before you get thrown in isolation."

Jarrod shifts his weight from one leg to the other. His growing rage is palpable. I swear there's smoke coming out of his ears. *Smoke and blood.*

"Have I ever lied to you, Griffin?" Eugene pleads. I turn my head and stare into his gray eyes. *He'll kill you like he killed 2.*

"No," I relent. "You've never lied to me."

The Watkins Effect.

"I'm telling ya true, man. Just listen. Listen to what they say on the phone."

The phone? No. He's off. Worse than before. I think his mind has officially split.

I pat his shoulders and smile at him. "Okay, Gene. I'll listen."

Eugene's face lights up.

"I'm gonna go show Jarrod around this place so he knows where everything is, okay?" I say and nod my head at Jarrod.

"Yeah, sure. Sounds good. We're gonna go play solitaire anyway. It was good to see you, man. We'll catch up real soon!"

I wave as they walk away.

Jarrod doesn't say a word as we make our way back down to our room. In fact, he doesn't say anything as we get ready to go to sleep. I pull the privacy curtain over and when I ask him what's wrong, he grumbles a heartless, "Nothing." So, I ignore him and hope that whatever he's stewing in right now will be dissolved by morning.

I say, "Goodnight," and turn out the lamp on my nightstand. He mumbles something, but I don't understand what he says. I ask, "What?" for clarification.

I hear him turn over on his bed. "I hate that nutsack!" he says with venom and shuts out his light.

TENSION MOUNTS IN THE HOSPITAL AS EACH day passes. The Infected grow hungrier, the humans grow wearier, and the Altereds slowly get pushed further to the edge. The edge of what? I have no clue, but it doesn't feel right. None of this feels right.

We're not prisoners. But really, we are—essentially trapped here on the inside of the hospital. Inside here or outside out there, neither situation is ideal. Now, it's all a matter of adjusting and adapting to the new way of life, the new normal. Survival of the fittest. And the only two who are truly fit for the world, whether it be inside or out, are Jarrod and me. Truly.

I fear Jarrod is slipping into madness, like he's standing on the edge of the beach, and he has one foot on the sand and the other foot is cautiously pressing his toes to the foamy water. I can't tell if it all stems from his outward disgust for the whole world or if there's something more at play. His tossing and turning at night has gotten more severe, and every morning we've been here, he's woken up to a bloodstained pillowcase. When he lifts his head up, the blood from his ear has dried and crusted down his neck so badly that it makes a ripping sound when he pulls it from the fabric. I ask him if he feels well; he just shrugs his shoulders and mumbles a typical, "I dunno."

But I do know because I can relate. I haven't felt well either, to be honest. I've been having the same bloody ear thing going on, just not as gravely as Jarrod, and my body feels at war with itself. It coincides with the war inside my head, actually. It's like hunger vs. sickness. The pains radiate from the bottom of my stomach and send sharp currents throughout my whole body. Sometimes piercing waves shock my head, leaving me with these little flashes of a migraine. Sometimes they shoot down my arms, leaving my fingers numb and tingly. They come out of nowhere and without warning, too, which is quite annoying if you want to know the truth. At first, I just assumed it was residuals from my hunger pangs—after-effects from the prepper feast—but now I'm not so sure.

One thing I quickly learned about this research facility is that Graves conducts pow-wows of sorts with the Altereds *and* humans. It's kind of a group therapy session for whoever wants to go, only they don't call it *group*. *Group* would indicate that it's a psychobabble meeting, and the last thing the higher-ups want people to feel is intimidated or like they're being evaluated or even tested on. But I know better. I know Graves. Graves wouldn't voluntarily give up his time to sit down and listen to Altereds and people hashing out their feelings. Oh no! There's always an ulterior motive with him. And even though he sits and listens and minimally directs the conversations, he's right in the thick of it with his clipboard and pen. I mean, this *is* a research facility after all. Psychology would happen to fall under the category of research, wouldn't it? I think the comfort and safety the hospital provides from the chaotic world has made Altereds and people alike forget where they really are and throw caution to the wind.

Dr. Oswald had suggested that Jarrod and I go to one of Graves's meet-and-greets. Said it would be "good for our souls" to sit around and talk about anything, every-thing, and nothing in particular. She said the meetings were always an integral part of the facility and were a good way to build community and camaraderie with the people we'd essentially be spending the rest of our lives with. She said if the social aspect of life is lost, we're reduced to nothing but savagery.

Well, I hate to tell her, but...

I don't know why, but I had agreed to go and prom-ised I would try to convince Jarrod to join me. Under one condition, of course—I promised myself I wouldn't let Graves slither his way into my brain again. *Ever* again. Oswald smiled so brightly—so *familiarly*—when I said yes, it actually warmed my heart. No joke! Like, this crazy heat flourished in the center of my chest and worked its way to my face where I uncontrollably had smiled back. I'm such a dork, I know, but I'm just so awe-stricken at how much she resembles Dr. Holston. Not in her physical appearance, but in her good-natured spirit. It's almost as if she sucked in his soul when he died, and he now lives on through her.

It took a little more than a warm smile to convince Jarrod to go. Actually, there was a little screaming, a little debating, a little arm-twisting, and I'll admit it, a little begging to get him to agree.

I got up early this morning and went to the cafeteria to get us breakfast, although I know we will barely touch it. When I get back, Jarrod is awake and cleaning up—not only was the pillowcase soiled with blood, but the bed sheets had some splatters here and there.

I put one of the trays on my bed and hold up the other. "Do you want any of this?" I say, lifting it in the air before me.

He shakes his head. "No. No."

"You okay? How you feeling this morning?"

"Fine. I'm fine," he snaps tersely.

"Graves's session is in about twenty minutes and…"

"I don't understand you, Griffin," he interrupts. "One day you're a stone-cold killer; the next you're like a trained puppy dog. What's your deal, man?"

"My deal? I have no deal," I say defensively.

"Sure you do. And if you can't realize just how schizo you really are, then you have far more problems than me."

I put the tray on the bed next to the other one. I remember lifting the cover of one of these exact same trays many years ago and staring at a plate of chicken cutlet parmesan. It looked like white, fatty fingers covered in blood and turned my stomach something awful. If I remember correctly, I may have vomited in my mouth a little back then. And now, even knowing what's inside the trays—a bottle of water, package of crackers, small serving of scrambled egg substitute, and a spoonful of soggy hash browns—my stomach jolts at the prospect of having to suck that down. I sigh loudly, exasperated. "Are we going or not?" I whine with a hint of defeat.

He wipes his ear one last time with a towel and throws it on the floor. "Whatever," he huffs and pushes past me and out the door.

My deal. I think on that concept as we head for the day room. In a way, it kinda makes sense. Deal—as in cards, as in a game. I've been playing this game for years now, and yes, the rules have changed some, but there will definitely be winners and losers. I think it's fair to say I have not had much luck in the game, because I'm still trying to figure out how to play. *All this time. All this time.* One thing is for sure, I've been fortunate to play from all angles—human, Infected, Altered, Changed, bad guy, good guy, both with and without moral obligation. In that respect, who's been luckier than me to have experienced all those different stages of the game? But having those experiences alone will not determine the outcome—*my* outcome. *That* I am still trying to figure out for myself. I wonder if Jarrod is, too, or if he's made his choice about his place in the world.

The day room is set up for Graves's session— *group*—and it seems as if every head swivels around in our direction when we enter. Eugene flashes me a toothy smile, and Crystal's eyes flicker to life when she sees me. Most of the circle is filled with unfamiliar faces, and Graves nods to two empty chairs, one on the opposite side of the other.

I sit down and place my hands in my lap, anticipating the sound of Graves's voice, anticipating the barrage of questions I know will surely come. Jarrod sits across from me and acknowledges no one. The people around me stare, and I notice there's a decent mix of Altereds and humans. I guess this part of the social experiment must be working out if Oswald and Graves have been able to gather the two species together amicably. A Hispanic Altered guy, who looks to be in his forties, and a black Altered woman, who looks to be in her mid-twenties, nod at me and smile in a knowing way, like they knew me from somewhere—from Before. I nod and smile back cordially, acknowledging some unspoken connection, but I can't for the life of me place their faces or remember who they are. They don't exist anywhere in my memory bank, but I play it off as if they do.

Graves rests his left foot on top of his right knee, forming the number four with his legs. He flips open his notepad and taps a black pen against the yellow legal pad. I eye him up and down, absorbing the magnitude of his presence. Uneasy thoughts race across my mind, and I'm conflicted with the question: Is he friend, or is he foe? He's always been foe. But does that mean he will always *be* foe?

"Okay everybody, let's begin."

The group collectively stiffens at the sound of his commanding voice. I hate to admit it, but I shudder on the inside, too. Instinct. Knee-jerk reaction to whenever Graves is present.

"I'd like to introduce Griffin and Jarrod," he continues, motioning to us. "They've been at the facility for a few days now." He flips back and forth between some pages and jots a few things down.

The group nods their heads. The Hispanic guy who seemed to recognize me mouths, "Twenty-four."

Jarrod puts his hand up in a semi-wave and bites his lower lip. He doesn't want to be here. Doesn't want to be on display for these prying eyes and Graves's analyzation.

"So," he opens the floor, "are there any pressing issues or matters that you would like to address? Let's start with any housekeeping items."

"The showers need to be scoured," a human woman says. "They're getting pretty gross."

Eugene lets out a huff of air and snickers. "Isn't it your week, Nicole?"

"No, it isn't!" Nicole snaps. "I've been in the kitchen. I don't know the last time any of the bathrooms were cleaned properly!"

Eugene laughs again like he doesn't care. It doesn't bother him; I can't imagine when the last time he took a shower was. Nicole breathes in and opens her mouth to say something, but Graves raises his hand, silencing both her and Eugene. "Enough," he commands. "Whoever does the hallway duty, you need to get to the nurses' station and put in a ticket for the bathrooms."

An Altered man with a small facial scar says, "Gotcha."

"Good," Graves says. "Anyone else?"

An Altered woman with long brown hair stretches her legs out into the middle of the circle and yawns. "What's being done about the Infected on the third floor? Are they getting moved? Am I getting moved? What's going on? It's getting worse each night, and I don't know if they're not getting fed or if..."

"It's you," Eugene blurts. "You're too close to them. They smell you. You're interesting to them, and they're curious about your smell."

"But the Infected don't eat the Altered," she crows. "Why would they be interested in my smell?"

"Curiosity, maybe?" Eugene answers. "Maybe they like your smell."

"But they're not gonna, like, eat me!" she insists.

"Oh, you'd be surprised," he whispers. "If those Infected are hungry enough..."

"Yeah, what about *your* smell, Gene?" a human man interrupts, and the circle erupts in laughter.

Eugene smiles and proudly brushes a closed fist on the top part of his chest. "Natural perfume, baby! Keeps the uglies at bay!"

Crystal giggles behind her hands, and everyone laughs out loud. I even see a small upturn on the side of Graves's mouth, but Jarrod is as stiff as a board.

"Alright! Alright!" Graves announces, waving his hand in the air, trying to bring order back to our group. "Last time we met, Ricardo said he was having nightmares about…" he flips his yellow pad a few times, "…canaries. Canaries that attacked you and your wife, correct?"

The Hispanic Altered who gave me the head-nod before shifts uneasily in his chair. "Yes," he confirms, with his eyes focused on the floor.

"Anika gave some great advice on how to quell those nightmares. Did you try any of her suggestions?"

The young Black woman next to him places her hand on Ricardo's knee and squeezes. "Yes," he says.

"And?" Graves probes. "Any of it help?"

Ricardo hesitates for a moment. "Yes. But now I'm not dreaming of canaries; I'm dreaming of food."

"Food attacking you?" Eugene exclaims with a chuckle.

Ricardo looks up at him and shakes his head. "No, dumbass. Food. Just eating it. Devouring it."

"And that's a nightmare? What kind of nightmare is that?" the human woman Nicole says.

No one says anything. I look over at Jarrod, and he remains quiet and still, with his arms folded over his chest and his legs spread wide apart.

"Let Ricardo continue," Graves says as he feverishly writes something down.

"I don't know," Ricardo says sheepishly. "I can't explain it. The dream starts out okay. There's a feast, a wedding reception sometimes, a birthday party some others. And there's this table of food—all kinds of food, delicious foods, high-quality foods. And in the dream,

I sit down with a fork and just start picking at all the plates. A little of this, a little of that. Until suddenly, I'm locked in a chair, and my mouth is pried open, and food just keeps coming and coming, and I can't stop it."

"Oh," Nicole says. "I can definitely see how that would be a nightmare."

"Is your wife in the dream with you?" Graves asks.

"Yes," Ricardo answers.

"Is she normal in the dream, or is she Infected?"

"Neither. She's something different."

I shudder on the inside. Something different like me? Like Jarrod? What the hell is Ricardo dreaming about? Are these some weird premonitions? Whatever it is, it definitely piques Graves's interest because he can't write his words fast enough on the page.

The circle goes quiet for a minute. "How is everyone else sleeping?" Graves asks, as he looks up from his notepad and breaks the silence.

Jarrod lets out a sarcastic huff. A disgusted huff. An angry huff.

"Jarrod?" Graves asks him. "Something you want to add?"

He re-crosses his arms. "Nah, man, I'm good."

Eugene glances over at me with a puzzled look. I shrug my shoulders as if to say, "Not a clue, man!"

The Altered man with the "barely-there" scar mumbles something under his breath, and every Altered in the circle clenches their hands.

"What was that, Kevin?" a human man asks.

See, the humans didn't hear what he said. They couldn't hear it. They wouldn't even want to hear it if they could, but we Altered did. We all heard the words. We all felt the words sink deep into our chests. Ricardo didn't want to hear it because he winced, and the black girl next to him, Anika, gripped his knee harder, as if to comfort him. Sensing a shift in the air, Graves looks up from his pad, and I realize for the first time since I've been back that he isn't wearing his glasses. Graves has been around us Altered, studied us Altered long enough to know when something is up. His senses are tingling.

With a faraway tone in his voice, Kevin repeats, "I'm hungry," for all to hear.

"Oh, lunch will be in a couple of hours," the human man assures. "I'm sure you can hold out 'til then!"

All of the Altered look at each other, knowingly. Even Jarrod. What Kevin said was beyond the scope of human comprehension. And it hits me ... they've all felt it. All of them. They've all felt the hunger and pain and panic and despair and struggle and want and need and craving. Not as an Infected, either ... as an Altered. And that's what made the Black Death so attractive to the Altered community—to be able to feel that moment for a brief amount of time. Every Altered has that war inside of him—the constant back and forth of moral human dignity and basic animalistic savagery. And now, with chaos right outside our doors, there's a sort of temptation to just give in to it. Why bother pretending to be human? Why bother pretending to be something we're not and never will be again? Why bother with the façade if we Altered are truly the dominant species? Truly. When the Altered tried to make our way back into society the first time around, we struggled, but now things are different. The game has changed...

Graves looks back down and continues to scribble away.

Eugene pushes his greasy hair out of his face and says, "I had a dream the other night about a dog."

Nicole, the human woman who is obviously repulsed by Eugene, clicks her tongue on the roof of her mouth. "Um… in case you weren't paying attention, we're not talking about dreams anymore, and…"

In an instant, Jarrod balls his hands into fists and shoots up out of his seat, like a bottle rocket flying from its holder. "Just shut up!" he screams. "All of you! I hate every single one of you assholes!"

Quickly, I get up and leap over to him. He flails his arms wildly around and pants so hard that his chest barrels out on every deep inhale. I place my hand on his shoulder. "Hey! Hey!" I try to say gently. "Come on, man; it's okay." But it's no use. A growl makes its way out of Jarrod's mouth, and he chomps his teeth at me.

Graves is there on the other side of him, restraining one of his arms behind his back. Crystal balls up in her chair and hides her face in Eugene's shoulder.

"Dude!" Eugene yells to me. "Dude! Look at his eyes."

And that's when I see it—Jarrod's eyes are crying blood. Thick, red globules pool at the corners of them and dribble down his cheeks. I look at Graves, panicked, and he calls for one of the guards to come over.

"One of you radio Doctor Oswald! We need to get him to isolation!" he commands.

They cuff Jarrod's hands together and lead him to the stairwell, kicking and screaming and cursing all the way—completely out of control.

Graves and I follow closely behind.

17

JARROD GROWLS AND SCREAMS AS THE guard drags him down the hallway. Two other armed sentries have joined this brigade and to the outside eye, it would appear that Jarrod has quite the entourage. Graves walks a few feet behind them, and I keep a safe distance behind Graves. Every now and then, I call out to Jarrod, "Remember where we are, Jarrod," or "They're only here to help you." Once I even yelled, "Don't bite anyone!" Because if he did, ya know, *bite*, then we'd have another Southold High School Safe Zone on our hands. The guards' fear of Jarrod smells kind of like Chinese food—wonton soup and boneless spare ribs—and who knows, but if Jarrod bites, and I get hungry enough, we might even have another Richmond Prepper Camp on our hands.

Graves isn't scared, though. I can sense by the way he carries himself swiftly through the stairwell and down the halls of the hospital. Concerned, yes. Afraid, no. He's worried enough about the situation to ignore me being there, that's for sure. His calmness in the face of a crisis agitates me a little, because *I'm* getting worked up—angry, upset, nervous, hungry—and I wish I could be as cool and collected as Graves.

We come to a heavy steel door on the third floor, and it opens with a loud sighing noise. A blast of air from within shocks the hallway, and a man in a white lab coat appears in the frame. He fixes up his glasses on his nose and looks around at all of us—at me, at Jarrod going wild, at the armed guards.

"Restrain and sedate him until Dr. Oswald can get here," one of the guards says, pushing Jarrod into the laboratory.

The doctor in the doorway stutters and mumbles something, and I can't hear what he says, which is odd because my Altered senses are usually pretty keen when it comes to things like that. Come to think of it, the guard replied to the doctor, and I didn't pick that up either. Everything sounds fuzzy—like I'm underwater. Like everything is swishing around in muffled tones. This feeling is too familiar, and a sudden jolt of panic shocks me. I look up at the florescent light fixture in the hallway and the ceiling spins. I blink my eyes rapidly to prevent myself from falling, but the dizzying wave overtakes me, and I stumble to the left—right into Graves's shoulder.

Graves narrows his eyes when I fall into him. He grabs my shoulders and looks at me up and down. "Griffin!" he shouts, but he sounds so far away. "Your ear!"

This time there's no mistaking—hot blood seeps out of my right ear like water from an open faucet, soaking the shoulder top of my shirt. "What are they doing with him?" I yell.

"They're going to help settle him down," Graves says calmly. His hands squeeze my shoulders tighter, as if to lock me in place. The blood from my ear drips on to the side of his fingers, and his black eyes look straight into my soul.

I glance at my blood droplets on his hand and then look back up at him. "Let me go in there. Let me stay with him."

Graves shakes his head. "He'll be okay. They're not going to hurt him. Let's get you to another examination room to have your ear looked at."

My head buzzes, and his eyes darken. There's a storm inside his pupils—a hypnotizing storm of grays, golds, and whites. I don't think I've ever been this close to him to actually analyze the color of his eyes, but now that I'm here, I can admire the flecks of color against the blackness within. His eyes are complicated, like cold, speckled granite. I feel his mental chisel chipping at the inside parts of my brain, trying to hack away the edges of my own granite mine. Before I am completely mesmerized, completely lost in his quarry, my ear opens up with a final *whooshing* sound, and the last of the blood comes pouring out onto his hand.

I jerk away from his grip, and one of the guards calls over, "Get that one out of here!"

I push past Graves and bang on the lab door. "Jarrod! Jarrod!" I peer into the tiny door window and see Jarrod strapped to a hospital gurney, with a leather restraint covering his mouth. Flashes of Plum Island flood my head, and I pound my fists on the door again, hoping to crash through the metal barrier. I have to get in there to help Jarrod because if Plum Island is rearing its demented head in my memory right now, I can't even imagine what he's remembering. I need to guide him, let him know he'll be okay, and try to convince him in some Altered sort of way that "biting is bad."

A guard reaches for me from behind, but with all my strength, I am able to avoid the arm-lock. Graves steps in front of me and stares. Rage bubbles up inside me. "Let me in there," I growl at him.

"No, Griffin, I can't," he says matter-of-factly, and my anger swells up to my throat.

"Fine," I say through gritted teeth. "If you won't let me, I'll go to someone who will."

I take a step forward, but he puffs out his chest and blocks my escape route. We stare at each other for what feels like an eternity. When he narrows his eyes and tilts his forehead forward, the slight wrinkles at the corners of his eyes resemble thin highways on a map. His pupils grow so huge, they eclipse the entire swirl of subtle color in the granite stone of his irises. I plant my feet firmly on the ground, readying for a battle. "Get out of my way," I say under my breath.

Graves doesn't budge.

"I said, get out of my way!" I repeat, louder, more forceful.

Still, he doesn't move.

"Move!" I scream, and I set myself back on the balls of my feet. With one swift move, I use my hands to shove Graves to the side. A twinge of shock hits me when I realize how easy it is to push through him—how easily overcome he is by my force. Maybe Graves has lost a step or two since I've first met him. Maybe my Altered strength has surpassed the great Lord Hades Warren J. Graves.

I eyeball him coolly like I've won some grand pissing contest, then I pick up the pace and trot down the hall.

One of the guards yells out, "Stop him!"

When I hear Graves reply calmly, "Let him go," I realize I haven't won anything or overcome anyone. He wanted me to push him.

He wanted me to get away. To leave.

Bastard! Again, he's psychoanalyzed me! *The Graves Effect Deluxe!*

I stop running when I realize no one has followed me through the stairwell and down to Oswald's office. When I get there, I hear her talking loudly. She says something I don't catch, pauses, then speaks again, as if she's having a conversation with someone, but there isn't a voice responding. I look through the window, and her back is turned to me, but she's alone, and she's yelling. The conversation is too heated for the good doctor to be rationalizing something out loud to herself. "I'm so close! I just need a little more time! Please! Do whatever you can to convince them that I'm on to something here!" She throws one hand up in the air and rests it on top of her head. She grips her hair and scratches at her scalp like a broken claw in one of those toy machines.

She spins her body around, and our eyes lock. White shock floods her face when her brain makes the connection that I've been standing there watching her. Red rage flashes against my face when my brain registers that she's holding a phone and speaking to someone on the other line.

A phone!

"I have to go, I'll call you later," she says and then drops the receiver from her ear.

She hesitantly waves for me to come in. "Griffin, what's going on? I heard something about Jarrod going into isolation over the CB radio, but..."

"You were on an important phone call, I presume."

She looks nervously at the satellite phone in her hand and back to me. She lowers her eyes. "Actually, yes."

My heart flutters oddly with a sense of hope. "Satellite phones," I muse. "So, there are other people out there. Other doctors and stuff, right? People working to fix this stupid mess. Again."

She nods solemnly. "The whole world hasn't gone completely to hell. The government is still regrouping, and there are minimal communications happening from underground. My uncle's people are still at the CDC, and I've been doing the best I can to follow the guidelines in the proposal he wrote."

The Policies for Disaster of a Biological or Biochemical Nature and/or Attack. Holston had told me about it. It was his great manifesto that outlined what to do in the event of a global disaster. So, his legacy truly does live on.

"Dr. Williams and Dr. Schultz were virologists and friends of my uncle."

I nod. "Yeah, I know. I remember him talking about them in his journal. I also saw a news clip with Schultz talking about the containment of the Zorna flu."

"Yes, well, they've been working with me, helping to guide me through the different possible scenarios of the virus. But with Zombaxin in the equation, everything has been so difficult to figure out. I'm not a virologist, ya know. I'm just a pediatric surgeon!"

"Is the president still alive?" I blurt out without thinking.

"Uh huh. They got the top officials to safety as soon as things got dicey. Dr. Williams is in Atlanta, and he has been overseeing much of the government activities."

"Is that who you were talking to?"

She pauses. "No. I was on the line with Dr. Schultz. In Germany. He was there doing research when the second outbreak took a turn for the worse. He stayed there to monitor the situation."

She pauses and looks to the floor. "Griffin," she continues, unable to look at me. "Since you're here, I might as well talk to you about what's happening to you and Jarrod."

I raise my eyebrows. "Okay," I reply apprehensively.

"Sit down. Let me explain."

We both sit on the couch in her office. She grips the side of it, as if to brace herself for what she's about to say.

"Whatever Trager did to you ... whatever he gave you, it changed you fundamentally."

"How so?"

"Your body is breaking down. I can only describe it as ... eating itself from the inside out."

"But I'm not hungry," I quip.

She chuckles quietly. "The chemical cocktail, while the same, had different effects on the two of you. Jarrod's decline, although a bit delayed at first, now seems to be at a more rapid pace than yours."

Drugs are tricky. There never is a definitive outcome to any drug-induced situation.

"What do you mean by 'decline'?"

"Madness. Anger. Rage. Even fear. These intense emotions will put you in an Infected-like state. The angrier or more scared you get, the faster your heart pumps the infection through your veins, and the symptoms manifest. Like I said, whatever Trager did reconfigured your genetic makeup. He engineered it so that eventually, a mere droplet of your saliva into the eyes or mouth or open wound of a healthy person would have the power to infect them."

Altered, too.

"I suspect that was his plan all along, though. I know your bites have the power to infect, Griffin. But I think Trager wanted you to be able to walk into a restaurant, cough or sneeze, and infect the entire establishment."

"And move from place to place, slowly infecting everyone," I concur.

The Ultimate Killing Machines.

"The bleeding you two are experiencing is a side effect of the drugs. Eventually, over time, it will start but it won't stop. You'll bleed out from every open orifice."

I shudder. Bleeding out sounds like a slow and painful way to go. "And that's how I'm going to die? I'm going to bleed out?"

She nods, but she didn't have to. I knew the answer was yes. I've been dying since I left Plum Island. The bleeding ear, the hunger, the unsettled feeling in my bones, my inner war, the confusion ... all of it—it's all been my slow decline into the grave.

"And Jarrod?" I ask.

She hangs her head. "He's long gone. This latest outburst of his was the beginning of the end. There's really not much else we can do for him. But you..." She looks up at me, and there's a glimmer of hope shimmering in her eyes. A soft smile creeps on her lips, and her breath seems to hitch in her throat with a subtle hint of excitement. "After looking at all the results of your tests, examining your paperwork from my uncle's tests on you from the first time, and after discussing with Dr. Graves your mental capacity, I think I might have a solution."

"Wait a second!" I roar defensively. "What on earth did Graves have to say about me?"

"Nothing but great things, Griffin." She gets up from the couch and steps closer to me, taking my hands into hers. "When he treated you, he was studying you. He saw the same things in you that my uncle did. Except, my uncle looked at *how* you ticked, and Graves looked at *why* you ticked. My uncle and Dr. Graves were a wonderful team when it came to looking at a person from all angles—mentally and physically. They both wanted to save you in their own way, and it's no secret they often disagreed on the methods, but they both had the same intentions. And when Uncle Peter asked you to watch over the Altered before he died, he made Dr. Graves promise to watch over *you*."

The weight of her words sends me flopping back onto the couch. That's why Graves automagically showed up in Brandon after Holston's death. He promised to watch over me. And he didn't turn me in because all this time, his intention was to protect me. He never hated me. He pushed me and wanted to challenge me, and maybe was a little resentful and maybe even jealous of me, but he never outright hated me. He had a super messed-up way of showing it, but after all this time, I see now that Graves did a double, triple, quadruple back-peddle on me. The Graves Effect in full force. I guess I got the hard-line VIP treatment after all.

"So, what's your solution?" I ask, after digesting my Graves epiphany. "Do you think you can cure me?"

"Troy's blood is the key to everything, but I think yours is the proverbial lock. Troy's blood will be able to counteract what's happening to you, but even a full transfusion wouldn't be enough. You will eventually succumb."

"What you're saying is I'll die regardless."

"Yes." She sits back down on the couch next to me and places her hands on my knees. "But, I think I can use the combination of your blood and Troy's blood to develop a sort of panacea."

"A cure? A real cure?"

She nods solemnly. "With a little manipulation of the two, I think we can develop a drug that could alter the entire human population. I've gone over the data with the doctors and ran some preliminary tests, and everyone is in agreement that this could work. They've been working with other world leaders and doctors on ways to distribute on a larger scale."

"So, you want to use my blood and Troy's blood to create a new vaccine, like the one Holston had for the first outbreak?"

She squeezes the tops of my knees nervously. I don't think she even realizes she did it. "Not quite. It's more than a vaccine. It would be a revolution of an injection. Essentially, the human race would be no more. No more Infected. No more Altered. No more humans."

I pull back. "You're talking about mass extinction?"

"No, no, no!" she quickly corrects me. "Humankind will forever be changed with this drug. It's the next step in our evolution. The shift will not be an easy one. Real change is harsh and visceral, but I don't see how we can go on living like this, either."

"Wait! You're going to make a drug that's going to change the genetic makeup of the entire world?"

"Essentially, yes. Not at first, though. It will protect people from the virus, and then the next generation of children to be born ... well ... *they* will be the new race. The new evolution of man."

"And then I would be cured."

She slowly shakes her head. "No. I'm afraid not. It wouldn't work that way."

"You said you need my blood. So, take my blood, take Troy's blood, do your thing, and give me the cure!"

"It's more than your blood, Griffin," she says quietly. "It's *all* of you. Blood, fluids, tissue, organs, even bone."

I pull back. All of me? No one's ever needed all of me before.

She smiles weakly. "But, you would be the father of the new species of man. *Homo mutata* is what Dr. Schultz said he will call them. Changed Man."

That's her consolation? Her "on-the-bright-side"?

"So, use Jarrod! You said it yourself, he's far gone! Use Jarrod's insides, then make me a homo mutant or whatever it is you said!"

"Jarrod is no good to us. He's near the end. All his tests came back the same—he's rotten. Literally. His tendencies for violence have destroyed his insides."

I'll be rotten soon, too. So, I'm either going to waste away from infection or donate my living body to science. My future is definitely not looking too bright right now. "And Troy? Do you need all of him, too?"

"No. Just his blood. But because of his age and size, getting enough will take time and..."

"That's why you need all of me. I have more to give," I say.

She nods. "If Troy was your age, your size ... then it might have just been a matter of blood, but..."

"I have more," I repeat.

She nods again, and the weight of her revelation hangs heavy in the air. "One thing I am sure of is we're running out of time. If we don't come up with something fast, they're basically going to pull the plug on this whole operation."

"And then what?"

"There won't be a *what*, Griffin. If I can't give them a viable solution, and soon, we'll be looking at global nuclear fallout."

ONCE AGAIN, THE INSANITY OF AN INSANE person turns out to be the God's honest truth. The Watkins Effect. Eugene was right about the nukes. So was that YouTube girl back in Richmond. Eugene has been right about a lot of things, actually, and I feel a little disappointed with myself for not believing him. What's the old saying, "Never judge a book by its cover"? Eugene and I have a long history together, and I really should have known better to doubt him like I did. He was right—he's always been upfront and honest with me, even if his nuke theory was presented in his outlandish 16 way.

So, basically, they need me. What's left of the planet's government is planning on total world annihilation unless Oswald and Co. can come up with a new drug—or, as she called it, a panacea, a "cure all"—that will ultimately change the very fabric of what it means to be human. Is that even possible? I guess so, because I'm far from human, and little Troy could very well be classified as an alien at this point. His blood isn't even your typical O, A, B, or any one of the variations of those. Holston designated Troy's blood type as H. I guess when you're conceived, Infected and Altered all before birth, you kinda end up *different*. I have a feeling Oswald is trying to replicate Troy's genetic makeup, and she seems pretty confident that she needs me to do it.

But can it even be done?

I guess when faced with extinction, anything is worth a shot. I suspect Oswald would rather see my body torn up on the slab than have to try to survive a nuclear winter. Isn't that the ultimate goal of any species— preservation? The male praying mantis goes off to mate with the female, knowing *full well* she's going to bite his head off after the job is done. Yet, he does it anyway; he does it nobly for the greater good of his kind.

But what about me? What about my kind?

My blood and tissue and organs and bones and fluids would be harvested and jigsawed together to transform humans and Altered alike into something new— the next step of human evolution. Altering the entire human population. What does that mean? What would that make me? The father of them all? The originator? Adam? Patient Zero? And what would that make them? Over time, would their physical appearance change? Would their brain functions be completely re-wired? Would doctors have to start from scratch with medical treatments for diseases like HIV and cancer? Or would the new *Homo mutata* be immune to such tragic ailments? So many questions. So many possibilities. So few answers.

She hasn't formally asked me to sacrifice myself for the good of all humankind, but Oswald's smiling sweetly at me and kind of batting her eyes with a pleading rhythm, and I suspect an official request will hang heavy in the air in T minus five ... four ... three ... two...

Static hisses as the CB radio on her desk springs to life. Oswald jumps up from the couch and does a skip-trot over to it.

"I'm here, go ahead," she says and releases the button.

"Dr. Oswald!" the voice on the other end screams. "Doctor, we have a situation on the third floor."

She turns around to face me and holds the CB tightly in her hand and close to her mouth. A waft of cherry pie smell drifts my way, telling me that the good, ole doc is a little anxious, a little nervous, a little scared, and a little excited. "Who is this? What's your position?" she asks calmly.

"Barlette. Isolation room."

I mouth "Jarrod" to her, and she nods knowingly.

"Okay, Barlette, what's going on up there?"

"Ma'am, I don't know for sure, but the doctors who were with the patient seem to be ... *infected*."

Screams of agony come through the transmission, confirming the guard's claims. Oswald remains calm, but her once steady hand quivers slightly at the prospect of an outbreak at the hospital. "What about the patient? The Altered man?"

"I see him in there, ma'am! He's hurt. The infected doctors are attacking him. Oh, Christ! He's bleeding!"

"Okay, Barlette. Listen to me right now. Whatever you do, don't open that door. I'm on my way up." She motions to me, and I get up from the couch and move swiftly to the door.

"Doctor ... I ... I have to help him!" Bartlette screams on the other end.

"No, Barlette! Do not open that door! I'm giving you an order! The patient will be okay."

I nod at her in agreement.

Someone bangs on a door on Barlette's end. More screams of terror and cries for help echo on the radio. "I can't just let him..."

"Please! Help meeeee!" a voice pleads. Jarrod's voice. I imagine his bloody face pressed against the small window of the isolation room door, begging Barlette to let him out, to help him get away from the crazed infected doctors he's trapped with.

"Barlette! Barlette!" Oswald screams.

"He looks really bad, Doc! I'm going to open the door. I have my weapon ready to shoot the others if they try to attack me."

"Damnit, Barlette! You keep that goddamn door shut! Do you hear me? Do you hear...?"

But it's too late. The door opens with a deep hiss, and Barlette repositions the CB in his hand so his transmission cuts in and out. I think Oswald holds her breath as we listen to the events unfolding.

"Oh, thank you!" Jarrod gushes.

"I gotcha, guy," Barlette says. "It's gonna ... okay ... take you to ... what hap...?"

Then screams.

Barlette screams. In and out. In and out. Static, then screams. Static, then screams. Static, then silence.

Oswald quickly flips the switch on the CB radio and holds down the button. Now she smells like barbeque chicken and mashed potatoes. Her fear ramps up something delicious. "Warren!" she says frantically into the radio. "Warren, where are you?"

Immediately, Graves's voice crackles back. "I'm in the isolation room on four."

"Are you with the boy?"

"Yes. Yes. Everything's fine. What's going on?"

"We have a breach, Warren. Patient X is loose. Dr. Kim and Dr. Harris are infected. The guard, Barlette, is either infected or dead, I'm not sure."

"Patient X?" I blurt out with disgust. Oswald ignores me.

"Okay," Graves replies calmly. "Let's lock this place down. I'm here with Troy, and we should be good for now. I'll stay on this channel if you need me, and I'll radio four and five. Stay where you are and secure your area. We need you alive. We have enough manpower to contain it. It'll be okay."

Oswald's hand stops shaking. Graves always did have the magic touch. "Okay," she says, stifling a sob. She places the CB back on the desk. "Griffin, lock the door and pull down the shade," she instructs.

I shake my head. "No, lock it after I leave and do what Graves says. Stay here. Radio everyone you can."

"Absolutely not!" she yells. "You are not going out there! You're too important to my..."

"To your work? Listen, they can't hurt me out there. Jarrod can't hurt me. He won't hurt me. He and I are the same—brothers. I'm the last person he'd want to hurt."

"How can you say that? He already did! Your face is still swollen from his attack!"

"Okay, let me rephrase that—he won't *kill* me. He doesn't have the heart to. And he can't infect me. You can't infect the infected! I have to find him."

"They'll shoot him, Griffin. They won't let him live."

"He won't let them shoot him. He'll infect every person in this hospital before he lets that happen. I'm going. I'll kill him myself if I have to." I turn on my heels and head out the door.

The click of the lock echoes in the hallway, and my super Altered senses pick up subtle cries and yells and screams in the distance. Hurried conversations. Muffled moans. Locking doors. Breaking glass. Stamping guard boots. Clicking safety locks on doors and guns. The sounds swell up around me and suck back deep into the hollow of my chest. They rattle me to the core. Jarrod will not only systematically infect the humans and the Altered, but he will free the Infected to help him in his plight. But why? Is he so completely gone, completely beyond reach, that he doesn't know what he's doing? Has his rage and hunger intensified to the extreme breaking point that there's no coming back? Has his body eaten him from the inside out? Something tells me no. Something tells me he is fully aware and fully in control. The Ultimate Killing Machine acting in accordance with exactly what Trager wanted. Jarrod is on a killing spree with a purpose. I open up the stairwell door and head for the day room—the last place I saw Eugene and Crystal—because that's where I suspect Jarrod will go.

I should have been a detective, for sure. My stupid, lazy-ass used to sit in the guidance counselor's office back in my high school days, and she would ask me, "Have you thought about what you would like to do with your life after you graduate?" And dumb me would just stare at her and shrug my shoulders. But, I thought the whole purpose of a guidance counselor was to *guide* the kids through those chaotic four years—to help give them purpose and some kind of understanding of the world around them. She probably should have given me some life suggestions or probed me about where my interests lay. Maybe she did. In retrospect, it doesn't seem relevant considering all that's happened. All I know is my stint as Holston's spy and my super-Altered intuition would have made for spot-on detective-ing because Eugene and Crystal are exactly where I left them—in the day room. I figure with Jarrod's outburst and all that commotion, the two of them decided to hang out for a little bit longer after everyone went back to their rooms.

The two of them are at a table playing a game. Crystal's back is to me, and Eugene has a wide fan of cards hiding his face. When he sees me from across the room, he lowers his hand revealing his goofy grin. I hurry over to them as he stands up.

"'Sup dude? Everything okay?" he asks.

"No. We gotta go, now. Jarrod went crazy, and I think you two are in danger."

"Is that why there's all that singing?" Crystal says. Singing. The Song of the Infected. The new Infected. The old Infected. The previously Infected.

"Yes. I gotta get you out of here."

Eugene puts his palm up and presses the air in front of him, as if he were pumping the brakes on a car. "Slow down! Slow down! We'll go back to our rooms."

"No. It's not safe there. We gotta go below."

Crystal fidgets, and her eyes fill with horror. "Underground?"

I nod sympathetically. I know she's been there before, just like I have. The subterranean section of the hospital was the old mental ward. Holston put me there in solitary once after I had attacked Graves, but my stay only lasted two days, if that much. Something tells me Crystal is much more familiar with that area of the hospital. "Just for a little bit. Just until they can stabilize Jarrod."

"But Troy!" she squeals.

"He's with Dr. Graves. He's safe. Come on. We don't have much time."

I lead Eugene and Crystal to the elevator and press the button. A familiar *ding* sounds, and Crystal grabs my hand and pulls me away from the opening door. "We're not supposed to," she urges.

Eugene throws his arm around her shoulders and guides her into the elevator car. "It's okay, Crys. We're okay." He smiles at me. I know protecting her is one of the better things he's ever done in this life. He probably didn't have a purpose before the first outbreak. Probably just bummed around, drugging it up, and robbing people so he could get his next fix. But then the world crumbled, and he met Crystal. He found his way. He made a family for himself. He brought some good to someone else's life and maybe redeemed his soul in the process.

"You were right," I say to him when the door closes behind us.

"Right about what?"

"About the nukes. Oswald confirmed it." I press "S" on the keypad, and the elevator begins its descent. Even from the elevator shaft, the song of the Infected travels faintly behind the walls. It's growing louder. The dominoes are falling, falling, falling.

Eugene snaps his fingers with delight. "I knew it, man! I knew it! They're gonna drop the freaking bombs on us and call it a day!"

"Well, unless the doctors can come up with something they think can help everyone."

The elevator stops and the doors open wide, revealing the darkness of the asylum. The scent of death hangs heavy in the air and envelopes us like a dirty blanket. Crystal tenses up, and Eugene lets out a "Whoa!"

"Stay here," I say, as I move forward into the darkness, feeling my way on the iron-barred cell doors, trying to remember the layout of the dungeon from my previous stay here. One hand caresses the cold steel bars, while the other swats the air for the hallway pull-chain of the fluorescent light. Finally, the rope of the light hits the palm of my hand, and I pull down.

Crystal gasps in her throat when the light sputters on. I can only imagine the wave of horrific memories flooding through her mind.

"Stay in one of the cells until someone comes back for you. You should be safe here."

"Will *you* come for us?" Crystal cries softly.

"I'm not sure if it'll be me. But it'll be someone we know and trust."

"Trust?" Eugene says slyly.

I give him a knowing look, and he nods. I usher the two of them into one of the cells and slide the iron bars, shutting them in.

"Why does it feel like this is the last time we're gonna see you, man?" Eugene asks.

My hand tightens on the bars, and I look up at him from darkened eyes. "Oswald thinks me and Troy can make a cure."

Crystal squeals again.

"It's okay. They need Troy's blood. He'll be fine. But me. Not so easy. Apparently, there's more involved with me and the concoction of her super drug."

Eugene leans in closer between the bars. "How do they know it will work?"

"They don't; that's what everyone here is going to be used for. The Altered. The humans. The Infected."

"Test subjects?" Crystal whimpers. She should whimper. She knows what that's all about.

"You can stay here, or you can get out," I say quickly. "That's up to you. You're not a prisoner here. But know this—if you go, you won't be able to get to Troy."

"Gene! I'm not going anywhere without my baby!"

He waves his hands in her direction as if to silence her. "Okay. Okay." He looks back to me. "And you?"

I puff out my chest with mock bravado. "According to Oswald, I'll be the daddy of the new *Homo mutata.* The Changed Man."

"Like an X-Man, dude!"

I smile back at him. "Yes, Eugene, just like an X-Man."

He extends his balled-up fist through the iron bars.

"Well, 24. It's definitely been one hell of a ride."

I ball up my own and clash it with his in a powerful fist bump. "It definitely has, 16."

"I'll see ya when I see ya."

"No doubt," I say.

Crystal and I share a silent goodbye. Her eyes fill with tears. They dangle heavily on the bottom of her eyelids but never spill over her cheeks. I pull back my arm, turn down the damp hallway, and make my way back to the elevator.

As the elevator rises up the shaft, the sounds grow louder and more intense. Jarrod has brought about chaos and havoc throughout the hospital. He popped the balloon of tension and let it spill out onto the once safe halls. The song is inviting, and I feel the war brewing in my heart.

Stop Jarrod? Join Jarrod?

Slap him back into reality? Feast at his side?

Bring order back and help cure the world? Enjoy the last of days in a bloodied frenzy and ride out the bombs?

When the elevator door dings on the fourth floor, and I see him standing in the middle of the hallway—his bloodstained face and clothes, clumps of someone else's hair matted to his hands, his eyes slightly glazed over white—my soul is ignited with a fire and drive I fear I won't be able to control. The blood scent engulfs me like a cloud of smoke, and the singing of the Infected echoes in the halls, echoes in my head, carrying me away on the dissonant melody, leading me to the swoon.

"There you are!" he taunts. "I was looking all over for you!"

I stare at him. I have no words. I'm fighting on the inside. I want to hold my nose so I can't smell the blood, smell the food. I want to cup my ears to block out the sounds, stop the song, prevent the trance.

"I wanted to see if you were ready to play," he continues as he takes a step closer.

I step out of the elevator car and the door closes.

"I can't seem to find your friends, though."

I wrestle with the intoxicating feeling. The blood scent is maddening as he draws closer. "Neither can I."

"Even the little guy. They must have hidden him somewhere real good."

I breathe in heavily. "Must have."

Newly Infected come careening up the stairwell like a pack of berserkers and empty into our hallway. They fill the space between Jarrod and me, whizzing by me in a blur. My hands are hot, like electricity shooting down my arms. My face is hot, like fire behind my eyes and cheeks.

Jarrod moves closer. "I couldn't fight it anymore, ya know?"

"I know."

"I couldn't fight it like you can. How can you do that? Doesn't it wear you out? The fight?"

I close my eyes tight as a wave of hunger crashes into my stomach, rocking me with pain. "Sometimes," I manage to croak.

"You're fighting now, but you don't have to. Ya know, I came here with you because I didn't want to be alone. I know you don't want to be alone, either. But this place is no good for us. We might as well be back on Plum Island, Griffin! You know it just as much as I do. We're not meant to be locked up in isolation rooms. We're not built to be tested on. We're the dominant ones. You can't deny that."

I force the pain back down my throat. "But to what end?"

He blinks his white eyes rapidly. "Freedom."

"Neither of us have much time left, ya know. What Trager did to us was like equipping us with a time bomb ... a time bomb that's about to detonate soon."

"Oh, I know. And I suspect I'll clock out before you. So, with what very little time we have left, shouldn't we do what we were created to do?"

Gunshots in the distance. Gunshots from another floor. Dead bodies pile up on each other with muffled thuds somewhere in the hospital.

"What is freedom to you, Jarrod? What does all of this mean for you?"

"Just let me go." He points to the window at the end of the hall. "Let me go out there. Let me be what I'm supposed to be in the environment I was built to be in."

Because he's done fighting it. Done fighting the preternatural instinct to run and hunt and bite and feed and kill. He's done warring with the human side and the Altered side and the Infected side. He's done fighting the moral battle in his soul and remembering what was and dreaming about what could have been. He's done mourning the loss of his friends and family, especially his sister, Margo. Freedom for Jarrod is to just *be*. Be what Trager wanted him to be. Give in and satisfy the very basic of instincts, the very basic of needs.

He chuckles and wipes some blood from the corner of his mouth. "We could rule this world, ya know. Even for a hot second. Cause man, I've seen you in action, and you're just like me. Maybe even worse."

In his murderous state, it amazes me how calm and collected he is. He is clear-minded and sound even in the light of his insane thoughts and rage, even when faced with the knowledge that his time is coming to an end. I don't think I could be this lucid. I don't think I could demonstrate such poise and cognition. And I think for a split second—maybe Trager made a mistake? Maybe Holston and Graves and Oswald made a mistake? Maybe Jarrod's the one they truly needed all along. Maybe 24 is the real monster through all of this. Maybe...

Gunshots fire from the end of the hallway. Too close for comfort. An Infected at my side falls to the floor, and I crouch down low, covering my ears.

Another *pop- pop-pop,* and Jarrod crumbles in a heap before me. A lake of blood opens up around his still body—red and black goo ooze from the bullet holes, the stench of rotted meat fills my nostrils. His opened eyes go completely white, staring at me, and his arm, still extended, points to the promised land—outside.

I turn my head to see where the shots came from. Graves's body sticks halfway out of a steel isolation room door. He reaches his arm out for me to join him in the safety of the lab, so I get up, dodge the Infected running in the hall, and shimmy around the dead Infected on the floor.

Graves heard everything. He heard everything and made his choice. He could have easily shot both of us down, but he didn't. He spared me.

I have my answer now.

And I know what I have to do.

HE TRANSITION FROM LIFE TO DEATH IS
swift. Seamless. One second, a person is living and
breathing; then in a blink of an eye, in the very next
moment, their candle can be inexplicably snuffed out.
Something that happens so quickly for the person experiencing it can often leave in its wake a lifetime of heart-
ache and suffering for the people left behind. Because,
let's be honest, death is only really painful for the living.
The concept of death always perplexed me, as there have
been many people that I've mourned for over the years.
I've learned to push the memories of those deaths aside
over time and pretend as if they didn't happen. It was
a natural defense mechanism, I suppose, because if I
dwelled on the laundry list of lost loved ones, I might
have gone insane. Only in images of brief daydreams
do I recall my sister Sydney's lifeless body tossed up in
the purple night sky. Only passing smells remind me of
forcing my hands into Toby's abdomen— begging me to
stop until she was no longer alive to scream. Only a certain *ding* of an elevator lift brings my father to mind—his
face so jagged in my memory that I have to jigsaw his
features together, and he ends up looking like a Graves/

Holston/Trager hybrid. They are all fragments of realities. Hopefully, the bits and pieces of what actually happened combined with the romanticized versions of those deaths will eventually diminish over time until one day they will cease to exist.

I could only be so lucky.

I knew Jarrod was dead when his body hit the floor. Face first, arm extended, eyes trained on me. His eyes grew cold and whiter with his death—the cloudy haze color darkened up like frozen ice. I don't know why that stands out to me, but for some reason, it does. To be honest, I can't seem to recall what color his eyes were originally.

Were they always glazy white, and I just didn't realize it until now? How odd a thought that is—that I spent months with this guy, called him a friend (for lack of a better word), and I never noticed that he had the eyes of an Infected person. Am I that blind? I guess a part of me had expected to see his eyes turn magically from white to his natural brown or blue or green or whatever normal color they were before infection ravaged his body. What will become of my eyes? Will they see peace and truth at the hour of my death? Or will they stare blankly into oblivion, clouded with infection?

To think of death, the actual process of dying and everything it entails, is pretty mind-boggling. When you stop to think about the systematic shutdown of the human body, the breakdown of the cells, and the disappearance of the soul—the great animation machine that resides in all people—it's a rather marvelous event on a biological level. It's birth in reverse. Come in. Go out. Ebb and flow. Some people even say that some cells continue to live on after the body expires, and that death isn't an instantaneous event but more of a process, like walking through a house and shutting off the lights in each room one by one.

Biology aside, on a personal level, death kind of sucks. The knowledge that a person you knew, loved, trusted, admired, or maybe even just had a conversation with is no longer living and breathing on this planet can sometimes be a heavy weight to bear. Especially if you had a hand in that person's passing. And thus, this is why I've become a master of deception to myself. Push it all away. Like it never happened. Like it happened to someone else, or in a movie I saw, or book I read.

The armed guards at the facility were able to get the situation under control. Jarrod had not had the opportunity to fully take over the hospital; however, many lives were lost in the conflict. I know Jarrod was on the edge—losing his humanity to the infection and unable to see beyond his own rage. He could have walked out, could have left if he wanted to. Even though he had his mental capabilities and wits about him, the infection prevented him from being able to analyze the situation. He was cool, calm, and collected, but the storm inside him only allowed him to see one way—the path of death and destruction. He would have killed Eugene if given the chance. Not just re-infect him, either. Oh no, Jarrod would have full-blown torn him to pieces if he had the opportunity, and it would have been so easy for him to do it. Jarrod didn't know Eugene, so there was no emotional connection. Killing Eugene would have been just as easy as killing the people at the Safe Zone or the Prepper Camp, but it would have satisfied his soul and placated his anger and resentment. Jarrod would have done the same to me, but I was off-limits. We were of the same breed. I think he needed me to survive in some weird way, like I was a replacement for his sister, Margo. In his mind, I suspect Jarrod would have killed Eugene and the whole lot in the hospital as a way to convince me to leave with him and run wild and free in the outdoors until we both dropped dead.

If he had lived to see Jarrod in action, Trager would have been so pleased with his behavior. Pleased and proud, like a doting father. Trager would have been nothing but disappointed with mine. Crushed and hurt, even. Jarrod wanted to do what Trager created him to do—destroy the world. And I plan on doing the exact opposite.

I'm going to save the world.

I know, I know, it sounds so stupid to say it or even think it, but that's what Oswald says will happen in not-so-cheesy terms. The prospect of my death bringing on the change of the human race is a pretty magnanimous one. It's otherworldly to think that I will go out like that. It almost puts the concept of death into a neat, little perspective for me, cause truly, if Oswald is gonna do what she's so confident she can do, will I really be dead?

So, there's no turning back for me. I made my choice and, really, both my options were rather bleak. But I feel good that I've chosen this route. I feel as if I'll get my true redemption for all the disgusting things I've done over the years. It makes the arduous journey seem worth it.

Oswald has explained the entire process to me in medical and layman's terms. Some of the verbiage went right over my head, but I pretty much got the gist of it all. They're going to use drugs similar to the ones they use in lethal injection executions. The first one will be a sedative; the second one will be a paralytic agent. While

I'm in a deep coma-like state, she will begin harvesting the organs that will be most useful to her while I'm still alive—kidneys, pancreas, lungs. I envision my body on the gurney, flayed open-butterfly-style, Dr. Oswald dipping her hands into my chest cavity and pulling out piece after piece. One by one. Hand them over to one of the other doctors and put 'em on ice! She assured me I won't feel a thing. She assured me I'll be asleep for the entire process, and at this point, it wouldn't matter to me if I felt pain or not. In a way I want to feel some pain. Pain would be deserved and part of my redemption. I got a little confused when she talked about draining my blood completely and then removing my heart and lungs. Not sure which will come first. She's not even sure of when they're going to give me the last injection to stop my heart, or if it's even necessary to do that. That's something she's been discussing with Dr. Schultz over the satellite phone. One thing is certain—my brain will be last.

While Oswald is prepping for my *extractions*, I have had some time to think and reflect and make peace with myself and the people around me. As part of my sacrificial deal, I made Oswald promise not to hurt Troy and not to give any prototype drug to Crystal and Eugene. Only give them the panacea when she's a hundred percent positive of the results. She agreed, naturally, and I believe she will keep her word. Honor is a strong trait in the Holston family. I don't feel the need to see Eugene and Crystal again. After the incident, the guards brought them up from the asylum, and that was that. I said all I needed to say to them. It is what it is.

The only person I wanted to see was Troy. I mean, he was my entire motivation for getting back to Florida. Everything I did, every action I made was all with Troy in mind—the special alien child with the curious blood and warm spirit. When they write the history books over and talk about this period in time, Troy will probably be revered as a god—a modern-day mystical figure. And because I had sworn a promise to Holston and to myself, Troy was always top priority. But, since I've come back to the hospital, he's been sequestered in isolation, with good reason and intentions, of course, and I haven't been able to see him, until now. Under the current circumstances, Oswald said it would be okay for me to go and say my goodbyes, so here I am.

Troy's hair has gotten longer since the last time I saw him. His platinum curls are pulled back into a tight ponytail, giving him a distinctly androgynous look. To a stranger, it would be hard to determine if he were a boy or a girl! His marbleized eyes beam up at me when I enter his room, and he drops his crayon, rushes over to me, and seizes my legs with all of his hugging might.

"Griffin! Griffin!" he gushes.

I bend down and scoop him up in my arms. "Hey, buddy!" I say gently and with a higher pitch. I bounce him twice against my hip. "Whoa, dude! You're getting heavy! And your 'r's have gotten so much better! Proud of you, buddy."

He giggles and nuzzles his head in the crook of my shoulder. "Missed you," he coos. The heat from his golden skin warms my neck and radiates down my arm.

I sigh. "Aw, man, have I missed you, too. You have no idea what I had to do to come and see you. Are you okay? Are they taking care of you? They letting you see your mom?"

He nods his head wildly and smiles a mile-wide smile. "Yes!" he declares.

I smile back. "Good. Now, I gotta put you down, or else you're gonna break my back!" I lie. If I don't put him down, I'm afraid I'll suck up all his warmth and decide not to go through with my mission so I can stay with the magic child. He giggles again, and I release him to the floor. "Whatcha working on?"

"Come see!" he says as he grabs my hand, leads me to his little table, and instructs me to sit down at one of the chairs. "It's Momma, and Gene, the sun, and the hah-pital." He holds up his crayon drawing proudly. There's a large rectangle in the center of the page—the *hah-pital*—and two stick figures on each side. One is in blue and wears rectangle pants; the other is in pink and has a triangle dress and curly hair—Gene and Momma. Big circle heads with dots for eyes and a dot for a nose and a dot under their eyes for their Altered scars. The stick figures have big, arched smiles on their faces, and their stick arms are extended to meet each other to signify them holding hands. In the corner of the page is a yellow circle—the sun.

"That's awesome, bud, but where are you?"

"I'm the sun," he replies matter-of-factly. Like d'uh, I should have known that. Because he *is* the sun: the warmth, the life, the glow from within. It makes sense to me that that's how he sees himself—as the embodiment of a celestial being and not an ordinary stick figure.

Yes, Troy. You are all that and more.

He looks at me suddenly and tilts his head to one side. Then, he picks up a blue crayon and starts scribbling something on the drawing. His tongue wags from the side of his mouth like he's deep in thought, and when he's finished, he holds it up again to show me. "Griffin! There you are!" He's traced over the yellow sun with the blue crayon and created another stick figure. Me. Where the sun was. High in the sky. Looking down on the hah-pital, and his mother, and his pseudo-father.

"That's me? Wow! You made me look pretty cool. Like I can fly or something."

He giggles, and the sound of his laughter fills my heart with a happiness that had been absent for so long.

"But now, where did you go? You were the sun. Now I'm the sun? So, where are you?"

A puzzled look sweeps over his face, like the answer is so obvious, and he isn't sure how to explain it to dummy me. "I'm with you. Together."

I pause to catch my breath, to stop my stupid eyes from filling with stupid tears, cause he's right. We are together. We will be together. Troy McKenna and Griffin King—keys to the human race. "Has anyone ever told you you're too smart for your own good?"

He busts out laughing. "Nooooo! That's just siwwy." He stops and corrects himself. "Si*ll*y."

"Nice!" I praise. "Who's been helping you with speech?"

"Docta Graves."

"Yeah," I sigh. "He's a good guy, right?"

He looks down at a blank piece of paper on the table and, in his mind, plots out his next drawing. "Yup. I like him. And Docta Oz."

I reach for one of his arms and extend it out in front of me. Bruised veins decorate his forearm up to the crook of his elbow. Track marks left by all the needles and all the tests they've made this little man endure. My face flushes with hot anger, and I try to control my body from twitching with rage. Sensing my rising fury, Troy quickly pulls away from me.

"You okay?" I ask, but the question is more for me than him. "I remember how much you hated when the doctors took your blood."

He nods. "Hurts sometimes."

"Yeah, I know. It's okay, though. It only hurts for a second, right? You're very important, Troy, and I promise no one is going to hurt you. That's why Doctor Oz gave you this special room. To keep you safe."

"I know," he sings.

"Good. I'm glad you like Doctor Graves and Doctor Oz. They're good. They'll be good to you. They'll help you and protect you. Like your Momma. Like Eugene."

"And you?"

My heart sinks. I shake my head. "No, buddy. I'm not gonna be able to."

His sweet face darkens with sadness. "Why?" he whines.

"Well, I have to go away for a while. Doctor Oswald needs me to do something really *really* important for her."

"When you get back?"

I choose my words carefully, because I don't have the heart or stomach to tell him that in less than twenty-four hours, I literally will not have a heart or stomach. "I'm not sure when that will be. It's pretty dangerous out there, and I'm gonna have to be very careful in my mission."

He exhales with a sigh of disappointment. Of *knowing*. And I second-guess whether my lie was believable.

"Listen, buddy," I say, pepping up my tone, "you see that picture you made of us in the sky together. Well, that's where I'll always be. I'll be out there somewhere looking over you and Momma and Gene and Doctor Graves and Doctor Oz and everyone else in the world. But mostly you. We'll always be together. You're my special buddy, right." He smiles at me, walks around the table, and plops into my lap. Wisps of his hair tickle my nose, and I inhale him, savoring his fresh scent—not a food smell like the humans, and not a rotten smell like the Infected—he has the smell of the sea, the beach in summer, collecting sand dollars on the shore, a school of minnows nipping at the heels of your feet. "Remember when you stayed at my house with Momma, and we played and watched cartoons, and you ate granola bars for breakfast?"

He bounces his head up and down wildly.

"We had so much fun, I wanted you and Momma to stay with me forever! I wish we could have had more days like that."

"Me, too."

"I'll always remember that time, Troy. Promise me you will, too."

"Pwomise."

I raise my eyebrows with mock reprimand.

He takes a deep breath, thinks for a second, and says, "Promise."

I smile with approval. "Perfect 'r'."

He pecks my nose with a loving kiss and throws his arms around my neck. Choking me, I can barely breathe, but it's but a small price to pay for this moment with the child I would have given anything to call son. "I will miss you, Griffin," he declares loudly in my ear.

I lift my hand to play with his soft ponytail and press my cheek to the side of his. The scent of ocean spray is right there, right in front of me, lulling me to a perfect summer day. In another life, I would have taken Troy to the beach to build sandcastles and dig up crab dens. I would have taught him how to boogie-board and be a strong swimmer in case a current ever tried to pull him out to sea. I would have, I would have, only if I could have.

"I'm gonna miss you, too, buddy. I'm gonna miss you a lot."

FITTING THAT I WOULD END UP IN THIS HOS-
pital room with the two-way mirror. This was the
place of my re-birth, my beginning, the origin point
of my Altered journey of self- discovery. The room is
white. Sterile. It smells like disinfectant, like strong,
medicinal, anti-bacterial soap. There's no stench of
death or bile or rotten meat. I wear a white gown that
leaves nothing to the imagination in terms of modesty,
and I'm back on that metal gurney. I wonder if it's the
same one I had been strapped to all those years ago.
There are tons of machines and monitors in the room,
and a small metal cart full of surgical tools.

Extraction tools.

I sit up and look over to the mirror. My image and
the world behind me reflects back, but I can see right
through it. I can *feel* right through it. I know there are
eyes watching my every move, and I surmise I will be
some spectacle come the hour of my death. I always
believed that the two-way mirror is a reflection and an
evaluation. Someone's behind there watching me, for
sure. The cold, hard stare is palpable through the glass.
I remember the last time I was in this very room, I was

being watched, too. Dr. Holston and his band of merry doctors kept a close, yet jovial, eye on my every move. In the beginning, I had been so angry, so enraged by the situation that I had contemplated going all *Terminator*-style on them. I had wanted to pick up the metal gurney and smash that ridiculous and intrusive two-way mirror. But this pales in comparison to the two-way mirrors on Plum Island! Good lord, were they something else! I'll take this invasion of privacy over Plum Island any day. This mirror with its hidden eyes is a piece of cake. It no longer upsets me, or troubles me, or makes me feel uncomfortable. I size it up, like I'm going to unleash my rage upon it, and use my Altered senses to try to locate just where the eyes are positioned in the concealed room. Then, I smile. And wave. Happily. Like a little kid.

The door opens, and Graves walks in. Or should I say, he glides in, and I think, *No man his size should have that much grace and poise.* He really is a manly anomaly. I bet a lot of guys wish they could be like him—devilishly handsome, built like a Greek god, suave, smart, *sly*. He smiles at me and clicks his tongue against the room of his mouth. "Oh, 24!" he sings. "Keeping it light and sarcastic to the very end, I see."

I let out a burst of air with a *humph*—something somewhere between a chuckle and a sigh. "Graves! Never letting me forget where I came from," I return. "So, are you here to take my last meal request?"

He walks over to the gurney. "Not quite."

"Ooooh, well then let me guess ... you're here on business. My last psychoanalysis session, right? But you don't have your handy dandy notepad! You wouldn't be here for a personal visit, would you?"

He raises an eyebrow. "A little bit of both, perhaps." He pulls over a small rolling chair to sit next to my bed.

I breathe in slowly. Graves and I have a long, checkered history, and if I had had to guess who the last person was I would have sitting down with me in conversation right before I expired, Graves would not have been a blip on my radar. But it *is* fitting, when I come to think about it; it makes sense. My relationship with him has come full circle, in a way. He was the first person I actually spoke to when I was Altered, and now ... he'll most likely be the last. How sweet.

Graves places his left ankle on his right knee and pushes back in the chair. "How do you feel?"

I roll my eyes. "Here we go..."

"Really? You're doing this now?" he accuses with a disappointed tone.

I shake my head and relent. "I'm fine. I feel fine."

"Have you eaten anything?"

"No. Dr. Oswald said I could only drink water."

"Good. But how do you *feel*?"

I scratch the top of my freshly shaved head, as if I'm trying to rustle up something deep and profound. I know how I feel about the whole situation, but it's hard for me to verbalize the emotions.

Graves adjusts the sleeve of his suit jacket. Even in the midst of Armageddon, he continues to play the part of the professional doctor. That's dedication. That's love of your profession and respect for what you do. That's one thing you can't deny him—Graves never wavered in *his* ethics or morals. If he thought something was wrong, you knew about it. He told you. Yes, he was the manipulation master, and okay okay, maybe he did bend some sacred oaths to get people to fall in line with his own beliefs, but at the end of the day, he was a man of principle, a man of character, no matter how morally ambiguous it was. "You do understand what Oswald and her team are going to do to you, right?"

"Yeah, yeah. You don't have to remind me. She thoroughly went over all the gory details."

"Gory details aside, without looking at the medical aspect of it, how does it make you feel? Think on a deeper level. A more existential one."

"I don't know." I clasp my hands together and think for a minute. What does this all really mean to me? Sure, I'm saving the world! Whoo-hoo! And everyone cheers! Sounds great and wonderful and all tied up with a bow, doesn't it? But I haven't really given much thought to the meaning of it all. The underlying factors at play. I've thought about death and my overall contribution to society, but I don't think I gave myself the time to process my emotions on the topic. "It seems too good to be true," I blurt out, and the rest of the words come pouring from my mouth like an opened dam. "It feels too good to be true. To have such a poetic ending where all is forgiven, and I am cleansed of my sins."

"Is that what you think you will accomplish? Redemption?"

"I guess. Redemption and immortality, I suppose. You see, religious people believe that when you die, your soul goes back up to God in heaven. Spiritual people believe that you are incorporated back into the energy of the universe. Non-believers feel that it's lights out. Death is death."

"What do you believe?"

"It doesn't matter much what I believe. But I'm comforted by the fact that I will continue to exist in some way. That a part of me will carry on for years and years to come."

Graves re-crosses his legs, shuffling them nervously. I notice he's drumming his thick fingers quietly on the top of his knee. The motion and soft sound against the fabric of his suit pants make me uneasy. It's like he wants to say something—something real and harsh and "oh- so-Graves-like," but he's holding back, holding his tongue.

Not fair, Graves. If you got something to say, just say it. You've never held out on me before...

"You'll take the drug when they make it, right?" I ask.

He shuffles a little in the chair. "Yeah. Of course..."

"How does it make you feel, knowing that I'll be with you forever?" I ask in a serious tone.

He pauses, and a small smirk turns up on the side of his mouth. I smile wide and think *Gotcha*! But he's too wise for my siwwy games, and we both end up chuckling a little.

Me. Chuckling with Graves. On my death bed. As if this life wasn't strange enough...

"So, what do you think about this concept of immortality? Of living on for generations to come?"

I pause and think for a second. "It's like this: like all the pieces that make up *me* will kinda be preserved. And every life that has touched mine, they'll be preserved, too. This moment in time will be preserved. Frozen. Mom. Dad. Sydney. Dr. Holston, Trager, Oswald, Eugene, Jarrod, Troy, Toby, Amber, Josh, Crystal..." I pause again. "You. Every moment from my change to my now. Every person who had a hand in my *becoming* will live on with me."

"And how does *that* make you feel?"

Suddenly, I realize something. I kinda have grown to love this game. The psychiatrist vs. the patient. He says the same thing over and over, and one slight variation of the emphasis of certain words makes it seem like he's asking a different question. Psych 101. But the tactic works, because he's got me thinking. "Ya know, for years I've battled with being Altered and everything that came with it. I struggled with the memories of my human life, and the nightmares from the time when I was Infected. I fought the plague within me for a long time. I grappled with my own personal evolution of sorts. I lived lifetimes in a short period of actual time— lifetimes that are now only fodder for nightmares. I used to be the monster hiding under the bed. I was the poisoned apple. Now, I get the chance to be the prince. The hero of a new story."

He sniffles and scratches his nose, but he doesn't comment on what I've said. Icy dread grips me on the inside for a hot second, and I think maybe I've gotten this whole thing wrong.

"If it's redemption you're looking for, you don't have to go through with this, you know."

Wait? Is the good doctor trying to talk me out of this?

"What do you mean?"

"You've already gotten that. You've been redeemed for quite some time. You've given so much of yourself that I think you've filled your 'Hail Mary' quota."

"But what about all the things I've done when...?"

"When they were beyond your control? When you were infected?"

I open my mouth to speak, but I choke back the words. What about the Black Death and Trager and the Safe Zone and the Prepper Camp and all the lives I had a hand in destroying? I want to confess all my sins to him and receive a true absolution, but he's married to the old narrative—the Infected were not conscious of their actions and not in control of their minds and bodies. No matter what I have said to him in the past, or say to him now, he refuses to let go of that conviction. His last memories of his son probably force that belief on him, and I can't blame him for holding on to it for so long. He had to put his own son down. I can't imagine what that must have done to his soul. So, I just nod my head in agreement. He knows I don't mean it, but he accepts the gesture as my final stance, regardless.

"Did it cross your mind that maybe this won't work? That maybe this won't matter?" he asks.

"Sure. I've thought about that possibility."

"And…" his voice trails.

How does that make me feel?

"And nothing, really. I mean, I know it can happen, but I have faith in Dr. Oswald. She'll get it right."

His eyes flash for a second. "That's a lot of faith to have. Heavy."

"I don't have a choice, and she doesn't have a choice. She told me about the plan for dropping the nukes on us. If she can show them she's got something viable to work with, they'll put it off. This isn't something she's going to half-ass."

"Remember, you always have a choice. Always. What if they drop the bombs regardless of what she finds? What if they…?"

The intercom on the wall springs to life, and a voice mumbles, "We're almost ready, Warren." It's Dr. Oswald. It's almost time.

Graves stands up from the chair, and we stare at each other for a moment. His eyes are swirling, raging. I can't tell if he wants to hug me or hit me. I don't know why he tried to cast the seeds of doubt in my head right before...

"Thank you," he says, and he outstretches his arm. "Thank you for making *this* choice."

I look at his hand, up at him, and back at his hand before I clasp it firmly. Even his handshake is God-like—strong and firm, yet loving and gentle at the same time. He nods at me, and I nod back—a knowing gesture of understanding and peace.

He releases his grip. "Good luck, Griffin." But his eyes are curiously sad.

"Thank you, Dr. Graves," I say, and with a half smirk, he turns and walks out of the room.

As soon as he's gone, Dr. Oswald bustles in. She's wearing a white lab coat and disposable shoe covers on her feet. She carries a plastic cooler with red words sprayed on the side, "Human Organ Transplant." Only this time, nothing is being transplanted into anyone; that cooler is for the extractions. She puts it on the floor next to the cart with the surgical tools and comes to my bedside.

"You ready for this?" she asks with a determined voice.

I nod my head. I don't want to speak anymore. I want to get on with this and let it be done.

"Lie straight and still. I have to strap your arms down."

After she locks me into place with the leather restraints, she runs her hand over the top of my head and looks down on me lovingly. There's a similar sadness in her eyes that speaks the same words to me that Graves's did—*thank you, and I'm sorry.* "I'm going to administer the sedative now," she says, as she holds up a thick syringe filled with a yellow substance. "It will relax you. You'll feel like you're in a twilight state. You might even hallucinate a little, but that's normal. Go with it if you like." She injects the needle into the crook of my arm and presses down on the plunger. "You'll be awake, and after about ten minutes or so, I'll come in and administer the paralytic. That will put you out cold. It will anesthetize you, as well. Your body might feel like it's jerking, but that will only last for a moment."

I look up at her and blink my eyes rapidly. I find it odd that for such a major surgery, shouldn't there be other doctors and nurses in the room to assist her? I want to say something to her about this, but the drugs have already worked their way into my body, and I can feel the serum overtaking me, calming me. I think I smile at her. She makes me feel calm and safe.

"I promise I won't hurt you," she whispers.

And I believe her. I believe *in* her. Just as I believed in Holston. I believe because it's comforting and poetic—that all of this wasn't for naught. It makes me feel good, like the belief kids have in Santa Claus, even when they know the truth.

I believe in you, Dr. Oswald. I believe in you, Santa Claus.

A rush of wooziness flows over me, and for a brief moment I feel, as if I'm floating, but I do as she said to do—I go with it. I ride the wave of sedation, and it feels so nice. I turn my head to the double-sided mirror and look at myself. *Really* look at myself. My eyes are a glazed white. Like cloudy porcelain. Hazy. Consumed with infection. *So that's how I look as a zombie?* The thought pops into my head before I have a chance to cancel it out.

I continue to gaze into the mirror—beyond my eyes, beyond myself, beyond the pane of funhouse glass.

Eyes are there again, staring at me, watching me. The room shifts, and slowly faces materialize in the darkness. Sydney, my mother, Toby, Josh—they smile at me. I try to lift my hand underneath the restraints to wave to them, but my efforts are fruitless. Holston, Trager, and Amber crane their necks from the side of the room. Holston nods in approval. My heart warms at his consent. Through the crowd, Jarrod stands next to my father. For the first time in a long time, I can see my dad's face—his actual face that I had wiped from my memory so long ago. Dad has his arm around Jarrod's shoulder. Jarrod gives me a thumbs-up. I blink at him. That's all I can muster. But the fact that they're here is nice—cheering me on, patting me on the back. Maybe they'll be there waiting to meet me on the other side—beyond the mirror. And all my stupid and failed plans, all my mess-ups and slip-ups and screw-ups don't matter now. Come to think of it, they had to happen because they were all integral pieces of the inevitable puzzle. All those moments in time brought me back here—to this hospital, to this operating table, to this *Now*.

The world shakes—violent and jarring, but it's not the shaking of the construction site or the falling of bodies around me from the cloud of purple smoke. It's me. My body. It's not the world that shakes, but my insides that seize up in their final convulsion. Oswald gave me the paralytic. It's a hot shot that courses like fire in my veins, like the rush of infection. My lungs and diaphragm contract sharply in quick, rhythmic spurts, like they are being clamped down in an oversized vice. I gasp once, and as I try to take in air, try to breathe in full, satisfying breaths, the spasms in my chest only dole out more fire pain. I look again to the mirror. To the me in the reflection. My eyes are completely white now, and my vision is distorted, blurry.

But I'm okay. The spasms stop, and I relax. Completely. The room looks jagged and shaky, so I close my eyes. The last thought I have is that *this* is my contribution, *this* is my sacrifice and my salvation. The journey I've been on has *not* been for nothing. The many different versions of me—the human, the Infected, the Altered, the Changed— have all played a part in the ultimate end game.

A blinding white light flashes like an explosion behind my closed eyes, and I hear loud voices calling to me in the distance. They beckon me to go to them. They sound frantic and wild and anxious. They can't wait for me to meet them. They are the voices of the ages, the voices throughout time, the voices of my brethren from days of future past.

So, I'll go to them because they need me.

Homo mutata.

This has all been for something.

I guess I have been lucky.

1. What do you think the title "extinction event" signifies? How does it relate to the plot? How does it relate to both humanity's extinction event and Griffin's personal one?

2. Griffin and Jarrod travel from New York to Florida and encounter many obstacles along the way. Which obstacle do you think was the most impactful on Griffin's development as a character? On Jarrod's?

3. How has Graves's role changed by the end of the story? How has it stayed the same?

4. Black Death has changed the game in terms of infection and transmission. How does the second outbreak of the virus differ from the first, and what impact does this have on the characters and the overall story?

5. How are themes of survival and desperation explored in the novel? What do Griffin and Jarrod's struggles reveal about human nature?

6. What does Griffin's concept of "home" represent in the novel? How does his journey to find his way home affect him and those around him?

7. How does the time spent imprisoned on Plum Island impact Griffin and Jarrod's mental and emotional states? How do their experiences there influence their actions upon returning to the mainland?

8. How did the ending of the novel affect you? Discuss the emotional impact and whether it provided a satisfying conclusion to the series.

9. Discuss Griffin's efforts to contain his infected nature. How successful is he, and what challenges does he face in maintaining control?

10. At the end, Griffin says, "A blinding white light flashes like an explosion behind my eyes." We know this to be the end of his life and the sacrifice he's made. But what if it wasn't? What if the government actually did drop the bombs? Discuss.

MARIA DEVIVO WRITES HORROR AND DARK fantasy for both a YA and an adult audience. Each of her series has been Amazon best-sellers and has won multiple awards since 2012. A lover of all things dark and demented, the worlds she creates are fantastical and immersive. Get swept away in the lands of elves, zombies, angels, demons, and witches (but not all in the same place). Maria takes great pleasure in warping the comfort factor in her readers' minds—just when you think you've reached a safe space in her stories, she snaps you back into her twisted reality.

Discover more at
4HorsemenPublications.com

10% off using HORSEMEN10

www.ingramcontent.com/pod-product-compliance
Lightning Source LLC
Chambersburg PA
CBHW061521310726
48972CB00008B/2285